# yours TO forget

# EMILY SILVER

TRAVELIN' HOOSIER BOOKS

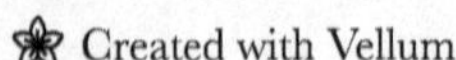 Created with Vellum

*To Logan*
*You deserve your HEA more than anyone*

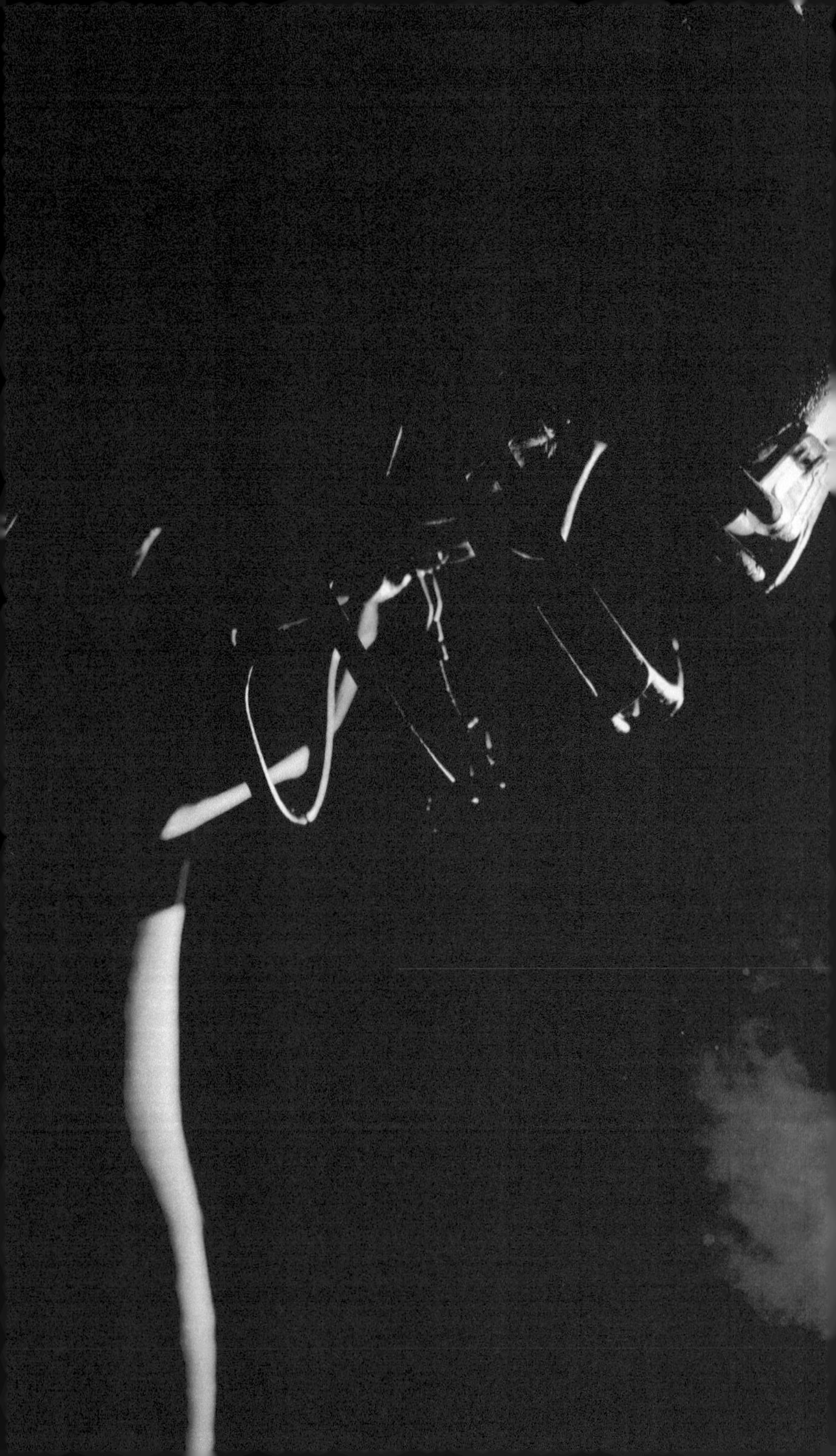

The roar of the crowd is deafening as I step onto the field. There's less than a minute left in the game and we're down by three. We've been here before. Nothing we can't overcome.

Except this time, it's the Super Bowl.

We've clawed our way back to be in this position. To give ourselves the chance to hoist that trophy as confetti rains down on us.

"Winchester. We're going to you." Our quarterback, Alex Young, looks me in the eye. "Think you can make it three yards?"

"Fuck yeah!" I yell. There's no way I'm not crossing that line into the end zone. I've worked hard to be the starting running back for the Denver Mountain Lions these last few years. I'm not letting my team down now. "I've got this, Captain."

"Good. Rocket Twenty on three."

We break the huddle as I watch everyone get into position. The crowd quiets as LA starts to shift their defense—

no doubt trying to predict what play we'll run. I listen as Alex calls the play.

The ball is snapped. Faking a pass play, Alex hands the ball off to me and I weave my way through the defense.

Straight into the end zone.

Touchdown Denver.

"Hell yeah!" Colin's lifting me into the air as the team swarms around us. "That was an amazing play!"

Running back to the sidelines, Knox Fisher, our esteemed linebacker, is hyping up the defense. Jackson kicks the point after, giving us a four-point lead.

"Can you believe this?" I swig a sip of water as the ball is kicked off to LA. "It's so close you can taste it."

Colin claps me on the shoulder. "We haven't won yet."

Nerves and excitement are bubbling inside of me as the defense stops LA, but not before they get five yards. Another couple of stops and we're World Champions.

The next play happens in slow motion. The ball is hiked as Knox gets around the guard to hit the quarter-back. It pops out and there's a scramble to get the pigskin.

When the refs finally pull players out of the pile, it's Denver that comes up with the ball.

With one hit, we're World Champions.

The Denver Mountain Lions are Super Bowl Champions.

Confetti showers the field in a whirl of black and yellow as families swarm the field. Every bit of it is chaotic. Hugs are given as the trophy presentation starts.

I don't think I've ever been happier in my life. Until Colin reaches over to hand me the trophy.

Except it goes right through my hands.

*What the fuck?*

I reach for it again and nothing.

Bright lights shine into my eyes, causing me to flinch.

That's when it happens. The field clears and I'm staring up at a tiled ceiling. Low humming machines replace the roar of the crowd.

"Logan?"

I try to shift toward the voice, but everything hurts.

"Logan? Are you in any pain?" I don't recognize the voices around me.

My throat feels like sandpaper as I try to croak out a *yes*, but it doesn't happen. I give whoever is talking to me a small nod.

"Can you give him something for the pain?"

That voice I recognize.

Mason. My big brother.

But why is he here? Wherever the hell here is.

The lights in my eyes start to dim, focusing on the room around me. Gramps and my brother are standing at my side, in what I can now see is a hospital room.

I try to move, but can't. Looking down, I see one leg is covered while the other is in a metal cage. I groan, trying to fight the swell of nausea that roars up in me. What the hell happened?

"Logan. Do you remember what happened?"

"No," I sputter out. "Water?"

It feels like I'm in quicksand, trying to find my footing. A straw is brought to my lips as I take a hearty gulp of the refreshing liquid.

"What happened?" My voice sounds foreign to my own ears.

They share a pained look before another voice enters the fray.

"You have a compound fracture in the fibula and tibia bones in your left leg." I don't recognize this person as I follow their voice. A doctor by the looks of it.

"What?" Everything is fuzzy. My brain isn't catching

on. The last thing I remember is halftime of the Super Bowl. Shit. What day is it?

"Are we in Denver?"

Gramps shakes his head, squeezing my hand. "You're in Jackson."

"Jackson?" Fuck. "For a broken leg?"

Mason scrubs a hand down his face, a concerned look etched across his features.

"The hospital in Denver discharged you. You were flying back to Dixon when you became septic—"

"Septic?"

The doctor nods. "You picked up an infection and you were brought here for immediate surgery."

"Surgery?"

"We were lucky to save your leg."

"But…" I lick my dry lips. "What does that mean for football?"

"Right now, the concern is getting you healthy again," Gramps answers for him.

"Football isn't our biggest worry right now," the doctor clarifies. "You will need a few more surgeries to clear out the scar tissue and repair the leg before you can even think about football."

"What about the Super Bowl?"

"Denver won, son. Thanks to a great touchdown by you."

"But how did this happen?" I wave a hand over my leg. "I don't understand how I got here. I don't remember any of this."

Gramps drops into the chair next to me, clasping his hand over mine. "You were trying to cut around a defender. Your leg twisted the wrong way when he hit you and it snapped. It wasn't your fault."

"Nothing you did wrong," Mason reiterates. "Nothing you could've done differently. Just an unlucky hit."

An unlucky hit. My leg gives a painful throb, as if reminding me that's why I'm here and not in Denver celebrating the team win.

I can't believe we won the Super Bowl and I wasn't there. Pressing the heels of my hands into my eyes, I try to stifle the tears that are threatening to spill over.

"Son, you're lucky to be alive." Gramps's voice is watery. "Whatever happens, happens. But we'll get through this together."

I was at the top of my game. The star running back for the best team in the NFL. And with one hit, everything was taken away from me.

Without football, who the fuck am I?

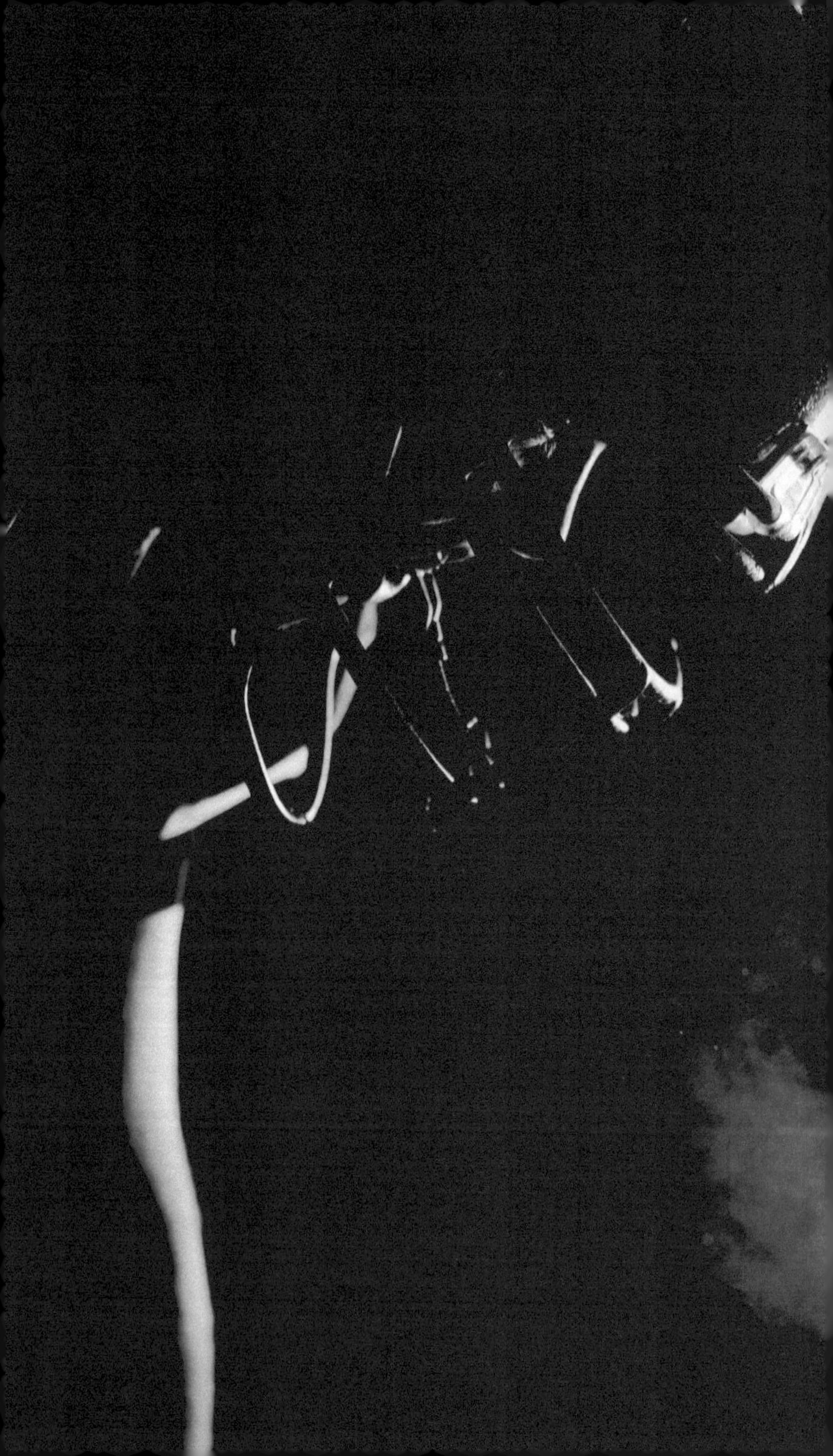

# Chapter One

"Three more reps."

"Seriously?"

Sweat drips down my chest as I try to muster the energy for another three lunges.

"You can do it, Winchester."

"I really hate you, Scott."

Digging deep, I do the last three lunges required of me before collapsing into a heap on the padded floor mat.

"See? Not so bad," Scott chides.

"Fuck you."

I catch the water bottle thrown my way and take a hearty gulp.

"You're doing great. Only a few more weeks and it'll be like you've never been here."

"Right." I sit up, draping my arms over my legs. "If only that were the case."

The entire reason I've spent the better part of a year here is because of my damned left leg. Permanent scar lines mar the skin there. It has a permanent tinge to it since my last surgery just over a year ago.

Longest twelve months of my life.

"Hey, you'll be ready for that physical in no time."

Scott has been one of the constants in my life during this time. With his bulky frame and tattooed body, he looks scarier than he is. He pushes everyone that comes into his rehab center the same. Without him, I don't think I'd be looking to head back to Denver in a few weeks to try and rejoin my team.

"You really think so?" I pop to my feet with ease. Something I couldn't do even a few months ago without my body protesting.

He claps me on the shoulder. "I wouldn't lie. You're looking good."

"Fucking finally. I'm ready to be done with your ugly mug."

"Aww. You really do love me, Logan."

"Who's saying they love you?" Scott's partner, Heather, ambles over to us. She's even scarier than Scott. With a septum piercing, one side of her head shaved, and a permanent scowl, she isn't someone you want to mess with.

Except I know better.

"Logan does. Think we could ask him to make this a threesome?" Scott laughs.

Heather gives me a quick once-over. "He's too skinny."

"Hey! I take offense to that." I squirt water in her direction.

"He'd snap like a twig," Scott says.

"Please. I've bulked up."

The two of them laugh as I show them my muscles.

"Whatever you say, kid." Scott pats me on the cheek as he walks by. "I'll see you for more tomorrow."

"I thought I had the day off," I whine.

Scott crosses his arms that are the size of my head.

He's right—they'd snap me like a twig.

"You want to be ready for your physical next month?"

"Yes," I grumble.

"Then you'll be here tomorrow. Have you talked to the team yet?"

"Left them a voicemail."

Scott doesn't say anything. He gives me an assessing look, trying to figure out if I'm lying.

Which I'm not. Not entirely.

I left them a voicemail last week to give them an update and then ignored their return call.

The thought of talking to the team makes everything I've been training for more real. I've been putting in the hard work.

I want to be back more than anything.

Yet, the thought still terrifies me because I've been away from the game for so long.

"Fine," Scott grinds out. "Don't go crazy with those brothers of yours."

It's the only thing I've been thinking about these last few months. Up until recently, every day was a struggle.

Surgery after surgery.

Learning how to walk again.

Figuring out if I could ever play football again.

Football was my life up until last year when one bad hit took it away from me. I've missed an entire season and now most of another one. Watching my team get knocked out one game away from a second Super Bowl was hard.

This year? This year, I'm hoping to get back on the field if we make the playoffs.

If my leg will allow it.

"Logan. You ready?"

The familiar voice shouts from the garage door of the gym. With it being a warmer November day, the doors are thrown open to let in the breeze.

In an old warehouse on the outskirts of Jackson, it's everything you'd imagine a gym/rehab place to be. Mats and weights everywhere. Mirrors to watch your form.

Scott and Heather have created something special here that athletes the world over flock to. I'm lucky I'm local and can work out here and stay close by.

"Hey bro." I grab a towel as I head over to where my older brother, Mason, is waiting for me before we head to the Tipsy Cocktail to meet Peter.

"How'd it go today?"

"One percent better."

It's how we started measuring my progress. Early on, I was frustrated. Learning how to walk again? Not easy. Every day felt like one step forward and a giant leap backward. It was hard not to get down about the little progress I was making.

Until my brother pulled my head out of my ass. Now, as long as I'm getting one percent better every day, I consider it a good day.

"Good. Ready to get some drinks?"

"One," I correct him. "I don't need a repeat of Saturday."

Mason laughs, a deep booming sound as we get into his truck. "It's your own fault."

"Mine? Nash was the one that kept making the drinks."

"And you didn't need to drink them."

"Reason has no place here, Mason."

"Whatever you say, Logan. Whatever you say."

We make idle chitchat as we head back toward Dixon. With not much going on other than physical therapy, I spend my free time helping my brothers at their bar in Dixon.

Staying here is temporary. A minor setback on my road back to the NFL.

I love my hometown, but this is never where I wanted to be.

By the time we pull into the parking lot of The Tipsy Cocktail, it's hopping. As one of Dixon's most popular bars, it's the place to be.

And on a perfect day like today? It's where everyone is.

"How was therapy?" Nash asks by way of greeting.

"Same old, same old."

"You'll be back to your old form in no time," he tells me as I slide behind the bar.

With how busy this place is, my brother's finally hired on more help, allowing more free time for him and his partner.

Without the two of them, I don't know if I would have made it through the last year. I stayed with them during the worst of it. My recovery was painful at best most days, but they never made me feel like a burden.

"Want to see the roof?" Peter asks, coming around the corner with a tray of drinks in hand.

"Is it finished?"

"Almost. C'mon."

I follow him up the stairs, taking my time. Nowadays, my leg doesn't give me too much trouble. But after a grueling session with Scott, it's always a bit sore.

Opening the door for Peter, I see the rooftop has been completely transformed. What used to be an empty space is now the newest bar area of The Tipsy Cocktail.

Greenery hangs from bars that crisscross above the space. Lights are strung up everywhere. A bar sits in one corner so guests won't have to go downstairs. Glass igloos are set up for the winter so guests can enjoy their own private space.

With the Tetons in the distance, it's the perfect spot to enjoy food and drinks after a day spent at the national park or meandering around town. The town is bustling around us.

The best part? It's only us up here right now.

Since my injury, I've been wary of people. Every person in town seems to slow their pace when they see me, hoping to get a look at my gnarly leg.

It's not nearly as bad as it used to be, but it's still an eyesore.

"What do you think?" Peter asks, setting the drinks down on a small table in the igloo near the door.

"This looks fucking awesome." I grab one of the beers and plop into the seat.

"I keep telling him that, but he doesn't believe me," Nash says, joining us.

"You have to say that because you love me." Peter rolls his eyes, grabbing his own copper mug.

"That's why I wouldn't lie to you. I think this is going to be great for business."

"Very romantic," Mason confirms, shutting the door to the igloo behind him.

"God, you're such a sap now." I shake my head, taking a swig of Peter's newest IPA, the Dixon Delight. Damn is it ever refreshing.

"You would be too if you had a new fiancée."

"I agree with Logan. It's weird seeing you smile so much." Nash points at him. "I don't think I've ever seen you so happy."

"Maybe you just need to get laid more…"

"Hey!" Peter tosses a balled-up napkin at Mason. "That's a dig at our sex life."

"Gross. Can we please not talk about this?" I wince, taking another long pull of my beer.

"I forgot our brother here has never had sex before," Mason jokes.

"Okay, fuck you."

"Speaking of people needing to get laid more." Nash points in my direction.

"And here I thought you were my favorite, Nash," I scoff.

"We're just looking out for you."

"Maybe once you're cleared to play again, you can maybe think about settling down." Mason eyes me over his own drink.

I love my family. I really do. But they are the biggest bunch of meddlers.

And I don't need any more meddling in my life right now.

"Just because all of you fools are settling down, doesn't mean I need to."

Mason leans back in his chair. "You sound like I used to."

"Okay, old man."

"Something to think about," Peter reiterates. "You'll want someone to grow old and wrinkly with."

Nash gives my brother a soft look. The same expression that Mason had when thinking about his fiancée, Ivy.

I had that once. The kind of love that I see all of my siblings have found. Over the last year, all of them have fallen in love and partnered off.

Not me.

I don't know if I'll ever get something like that again.

Grabbing my drink, I swallow down half of it in one quick gulp.

I hate thinking about that.

About her.

What we had burned bright.

And we went up in flames just as fast.

It's why the only things in my life are football and family. I don't need anything else.

Because once you've had the love of a lifetime, nothing else can compare.

I guess I'll just grow old and wrinkly on my own.

# Chapter Two

## AUDREY

Wind whips around me as I swish down the mountain.

This is what I live for. It feels like I'm flying. Nothing is in my way as I twist my body to hit each gate.

With the snow last night, it's the perfect run as I sail across the finish line.

"Great time, Audrey. Keep doing that and you'll be a shoo-in for the games."

Pulling off my helmet, I shake my hair out. "Don't jinx it."

Even though I'm feeling better than ever after a knee injury, I still have a few weeks of rest and rehab to go.

Runs like today though, where I make the mountain my bitch, feel good. Great, even. At the ripe old age of thirty-five, I know my days in this sport are numbered.

It's getting younger and faster. I only hope that I'm putting in the work to qualify for one more Olympics.

Heading back to the training center, a flash of a camera blinds me. Dark spots blur my vision.

"Audrey. How is your training coming? Think you'll qualify for the games?"

Trent, an obnoxious reporter from one of the sports rag magazines, shoves a recorder in my face.

"No comment." I grit my teeth, trying to get away from this guy and his camera. No matter which way I turn, he's there.

Been there since I started rehab on my knee all those months ago.

He's like a dog with a bone—won't stop until he gets the tiniest bit of scoop. And then he'll run with it for months.

I hate this guy.

"Are you not going to represent your team?"

"I said no comment."

"That's no way to treat the team that's been so good to you all these years. Quitting right before the games?"

*Deep breaths.*

Don't bite back at this guy. It'll only give him more ammunition to use against me.

"No comment."

I grab the door, but he's quick to stop me. This close, his brown eyes are menacing.

I really do hate this guy. Worse than all the other press combined.

"One quote. That's all I need."

"Then how about no comment?"

I break past him, finding a blissfully empty ski center. Quiet. Unusual, but a welcome respite from the chaos of dealing with that guy. This is the one place reporters aren't allowed. I'm surprised the douche actually respects the boundaries of this building.

I don't mind the occasional reporter. I have to deal with them in my position on the ski team.

It doesn't mean I have to like it.

This is one of the downsides of training here. Reporters from every sports outlet camp out here in the lead-up to the games. They're bloodhounds, sniffing out any hint of gossip or story. They live for the drama.

Sure, my other teammates provide fodder for their stories, but not me.

Ski, rest, repeat. It's been like that for the last few years.

Some might say my life is too one-dimensional. I don't care. After the heartache I've been through, I'm fine being on my own. I'm not ready to open myself up to that kind of pain again.

"Meyers! Coach wants to see you in his office," an assistant calls out to me.

"Sure thing."

I head to the locker room to drop off my gear and strip out of my outer layers before heading to meet my coach. Before, this would have stressed me out—almost like getting called to the principal's office. Ever since I tore my ACL on the slopes, I'm in here at least once a week.

Nothing to stress about now.

"Hey, Coach." I drop into the chair opposite his desk.

"Audrey. How's the leg feeling?"

"Good. Had a great day out on the mountain."

He adjusts his glasses. "Good, good. And everything else going okay with training?"

"Other than a camera being shoved in my face every day…"

I don't know where all this interest came from, following my road back to the games this coming February. Being in the spotlight has never been my interest.

This place is a second home. It's all I've ever known. Being raised in nearby Golden, the mountains here were where I spent most of my childhood. I've been training here since I was eighteen. Like with everything though, the new skiers are getting younger and younger.

And I feel like the old lady of the group.

"Everyone loves a good comeback story, Audrey. If you medal, you'd be the oldest female US skier to place in the games."

There's that age talk again.

"It's just a number. I feel good, Coach. I just wish I had some peace and quiet every now and then."

He eyes me, giving me an assessing stare. "What would you say to getting out of Copper Mountain?"

"What do you mean?"

"I've got a good trainer I could send you to. Get you out of the thick of things if you want?"

"Really?" That grabs my attention.

He nods his head. Coach Anglia is only a few years older than I am. One of the most prolific skiers in men's history, he took the job after he retired at the age of thirty.

It's still hard to wrap my head around the fact that he's only five years older than I am. Here I am still skiing at thirty-five, not quite ready to give the sport up. I'm well past the age of retirement.

"I can send you up to Jackson. Great skiing, quiet little town. No one would bother you up there."

"Unless they find out I'm leaving."

"We can help with that," he assures me.

"Are you sure?"

Hearing the town of Jackson brings back a lot of painful memories for me. Ones that, while they weren't painful before, have my heart clattering around in my chest.

All because of one man. One man I don't want to be thinking about right now.

"It's not going to do anyone any good if you're not in

the right headspace to compete. Go. I'll give my buddy Scott a call and let him know you're coming up."

"Thanks, Coach."

He goes back to his computer, dismissing me and ending our conversation. Not wanting to stick around, I fire off a text to my roommate, Lily, to see if she's home.

I met her when I moved to Switzerland a few years back. She's several years younger than I am and joined the Olympic team later than most. But we became fast friends—her not knowing anybody over there and me nursing a broken heart. We both moved back here at the same time, and she's one of the few people I've let in.

It's hard to know who likes you for you, and who wants a piece of your fame. Lily is one of the most genuine people I know. I love her to pieces.

The training center is now full of chaos with the slopes shutting down. This is what I'm used to. People coming and going. Skis being worked on. The loud videos welcoming you here.

Zipping my coat up to my chin, I walk the short distance back to my cabin. My thoughts are rioting.

Do I want to get out of here and leave the craziness behind? Yes.

Do I want to be away from shouted questions from the stalker press when I'm trying to get back to form? Also yes.

But…do I want to go to Jackson?

I haven't thought about *him* in months. Every time I do, the thoughts are too painful. I went to Jackson to visit him and his family so many times that Jackson feels like a home away from home.

But it's also his. He lived a short drive from there, so I know the area well. Would it feel like I'm intruding on his territory by going?

It's a big enough town. Surely I can be in and out of there in a few weeks with my heart intact, right?

With the late afternoon sun dropping behind the mountains, it gets cold fast. Cutting across Main Street, I rush through the door of my cabin to find Lily drinking a glass of wine in the living room with a roaring fire.

The cabin isn't much. Two small rooms joined by the living room and kitchen. But the stone fireplace in the middle is what makes it cozy.

"Hey. How was your meeting?" she asks.

"I need something to drink."

"That good?" she calls out after me.

Shrugging out of my coat, the heat of the fire hits me. The temps in the mountains are dropping, getting colder than normal much faster. With the cutting wind, it's going to make for some hard days of skiing.

Whipping up a hot chocolate, I add a shot of Bailey's. It's my favorite drink, but I only allow myself to indulge in it once a week while training.

"It was interesting."

"Why interesting?"

I drop down onto the small couch next to Lily.

"I'm going to finish my rehab in Wyoming."

Lily knows all about my history with Logan. Even just having to tell her this is going to stir up so many feelings. Feelings I thought I was done with.

"Wyoming? Why Wyoming?"

"Because the pressure here is too much for me."

"Did that dick come sniffing around again?"

"He's always around."

"And you're just going to leave me here? To go…where exactly in Wyoming?"

"Jackson."

"Wait. You're going to Jackson?"

"Uh-huh."

"Logan's there."

I wince as she says his name. Apparently I'm not as over him as I thought. Because it shouldn't hurt to hear his name, right?

"We don't know that."

"But what if he is?"

I gulp down a mouthful of hot chocolate, needing it to soothe my fraying nerves.

"I have no idea where he is."

"You mean to tell me you haven't been keeping tabs on him lately?" The way she cocks her eyebrow at me tells me she knows it's a lie.

"Right now? No."

Last year? Yes.

So not a total lie.

Even though I hadn't talked to him in ages, I couldn't help but watch him in the Super Bowl. It was his dream. And watching him take that hit?

It took everything I had in me not to call him and see how he was doing. I knew he'd be rehabbing, so I let him be. Pushed all news of him to the side.

Especially after I suffered from my own injury. That took all of my focus.

"Let me get this straight. You're just going to flit into Jackson, finish your rehab program, and then flit on out like it's no big deal?"

"Right. No big deal."

Maybe if I keep saying it to myself, it won't be.

"Bullshit."

I snort over the sip I just took. "You can't call bullshit. It's the truth."

"I don't believe you." Lily flips her long blonde hair behind her shoulders. It used to match my own. Until I decided enough was enough and got over my heartbreak by dying my hair dark brown. "I don't even know Logan, and I have feelings on this. It's a big deal."

This is one of the reasons I love Lily. She's been there for me since the day I met her. When you meet someone and you're a blubbering mess and they still love you? It's hard not to become friends for life.

"Anything has to be better than here, right?"

As much as I love Copper Mountain, I need a break. It's hard to get back into the swing of things when the race that nearly cost me my career is shoved in my face on a daily basis.

"Do you need some company? Maybe I can head up there with you?"

I pull Lily in for a hug. "I promise, I'll be okay."

"You're really going to leave me?" she huffs out.

"Only for a few weeks. You saw my run yesterday."

"You kicked ass. If I didn't love you so much, I'd hate you."

"And when you see me in a few more weeks, I'll be even better."

"You'll be the one to beat. I know it."

Sometimes it can be hard being around other athletes. You never know if you're going to be competing for the same spot in a race. As much as it's an individual sport, it's also a team sport. And sometimes it's hard to get on board when someone does better than you.

Thankfully, Lily and I don't race in the same events. We're each other's loudest cheerleaders on the mountain.

I have a feeling I'm going to need a lot of her cheering on over these next few weeks.

Because what if I run into Logan?

He didn't just break my heart all those years ago. He decimated it. One day he was there, and the next I was on a plane to Switzerland getting sympathetic looks from the flight attendants because I couldn't stop crying.

My heart hitches in my chest thinking about those days. I can't go back to that. It took a long time to feel whole again. To feel like the pieces of me were taped back together.

It'll be fine.

Ever since he left me, I've kept my heart under lock and key. I've given it to no one. Self-preservation and all that.

I'll be able to handle a few weeks in Jackson. No press. No recorders shoved in my face.

Because with a clear head, I'll be able to focus on my final goal. On why I'm there.

A gold medal.

Logan Winchester and everything else will be forgotten.

"**D**o you need anything else before landing? We should be on the ground shortly."

"No, thank you." I pass off my empty cup to the flight attendant and pull up the window shade.

The farmland is barren beneath the plane, but snow blankets the mountains. The closer we get to landing, the further my heart jumps into my throat.

I've never been a nervous flier. But I'm nervous about where I'm going. No matter what I told everyone back at home.

Coming back to Jackson is messing with my head.

This was always Logan's place. His territory. I feel like I shouldn't be coming here. But I can't keep going the way I have been in Copper Mountain.

The fucking press are just waiting for the merest hint of a story. It's not something I want to deal with.

Thankfully I was able to sneak out of town without anyone finding out.

Which means I can train in peace without Trent

finding me here. Without him constantly hounding me for a quote. I'm not sure how many times I can get away with no comment before he becomes even more aggressive.

The pilot's voice comes over the intercom as seatbelts are fastened and tray tables are stowed.

Pushing the thought of the press out of my mind, I try to focus on the task at hand.

*I can do this.*

I've faced down some of the scariest mountains in whiteout conditions. Who says I'm going to see Logan here?

I'm a badass. I've won a gold medal. Hell, two gold medals.

I'm not going to let something like the potential of seeing my ex get in the way of the amazing opportunity I have here.

I'm lucky to be able to come here and work with one of the best in the industry. Someone to keep pushing me to get better and better.

I surge forward as the plane kisses the runway, slowing down as the small airport comes into view. I grab my carry-on and am one of the first ones off the plane.

There are only a few gates here, so it's not hard to find my baggage claim.

It's nice here—no wandering eyes looking at me like they might know who I am. Everyone is always trying to find someone they know at Copper Mountain.

This is going to be good for me.

The luggage carousel keeps turning, fewer and fewer bags, with mine not in sight. It's then I notice a mop of brown hair standing farther down the line. His back is to me, but it sends a shot of awareness through me.

Oh shit.

He's the right height. Same build.

What are the fucking chances that Logan would be here, waiting for bags at the same place I am? Would it be bad to abandon my bags and come back later?

There's no way I can have a conversation with him right now.

It happens in a split second. It's like he can feel my stare beating into the back of his head as he turns ever so slightly.

"Holy shit." I duck into the closest open doorway. I don't want to see if he saw me dart out of there. My heart is pounding in my chest, mouth as dry as the desert as I wait for this feeling to pass.

It couldn't have been him, right?

I'm hiding away like a little kid. I'm a grown-up and I should be able to handle dealing with my ex. Not hiding out in some room in the airport.

"Umm, excuse me?" The deep voice of a man startles me.

Spinning on my heel, my eyes go wide.

Not just any room, apparently.

The men's bathroom.

"Oh God." Two men are standing at the urinals while another is looking at me like I'm an idiot.

"This is the men's room, ma'am."

"Right. I'm so sorry. Tired is all," I try explaining myself to them. "Long flight."

It was less than a two-hour flight, but they don't know that. Nor is this the time to try and launch into a made-up story.

"Can you leave so I can take care of business?" one of the men throws over his shoulder. "I can't take a whiz with a lady here."

"Yup. Sorry."

I've turned into a bumbling idiot.

Rounding the divider of the restroom, I peek my head around the corner. There's no sign of anyone at the baggage claim.

Thank God.

One of the men gives me a funny look as he leaves the bathroom, and I hurry off in the direction to try and find my bag.

*So much for being a badass.*

I cowered at the first sign of him.

The carousel has stopped, and my lone orange bag is the only one sitting there. There's no one else around to witness my humiliation.

I can't believe—of all places—I ended up in the men's bathroom.

I have too much nervous energy to do anything productive. Making a decision, I pick up my rental car and plug in the address for the gym.

Nothing like a hard workout to get rid of these feelings of inadequacy.

I clear my head as I drive into town, following the voice of my navigation. It's hard not to smile as I come down the main drag.

Everything here is exactly the same as I remember. The antler arches. People coming and going throughout the town, some looking like they just came from the slopes.

It's the epitome of a small ski town. And I love it.

And so far, not a single reporter in sight.

It's bliss.

The gym comes into view as I roll through town. An old, converted warehouse, it's exactly what a gym like this should be.

Grabbing my backpack, I lock my car and head inside.

It's crowded, even for the middle of the afternoon during the week. Sweat and hard work clings to the air in here. High beams allow for a lot of light to filter through the open windows. Machines take up one-half of the space, while mats and free weights line the other.

I know this is exactly the place I need to be.

"Hey there. Can I help you?" someone asks from behind the front desk.

"Hi. I'm not supposed to be here until tomorrow, but I'm Audrey Meyers."

She comes around the desk. "Scott said you'd be joining us. Welcome. I'm Heather, his partner in crime."

"Nice to meet you."

"I'll see if I can find him, and then maybe you two can get started?"

"That sounds great."

As an athlete, I gravitate to places like this. This is where I need to be in order to have a clear head. Nothing is more detrimental to my runs than getting lost in a bad headspace.

A place like this gym? It helps clear up the fog.

Fog that's been ever present since I started training again back home.

"Audrey. It's nice to meet you."

A bulky man with no hair and covered in tattoos greets me. "Hi. Scott, I take it?"

"That's me. I'm glad Oliver sent you my way."

"I'm happy it worked out. Any chance I can get started today?"

"Fuck, yeah."

"Scott. Maybe watch the swearing around the new people?" the woman at the desk chides him.

I laugh. "It's okay. A few fucks won't scare me off."

It's then I hear a familiar voice that stops me. Except now, there is nowhere to hide.

"Audrey?"

No. No way.

Logan? Here?

Is it too late to find a men's room to hide in?

"Is that really you?"

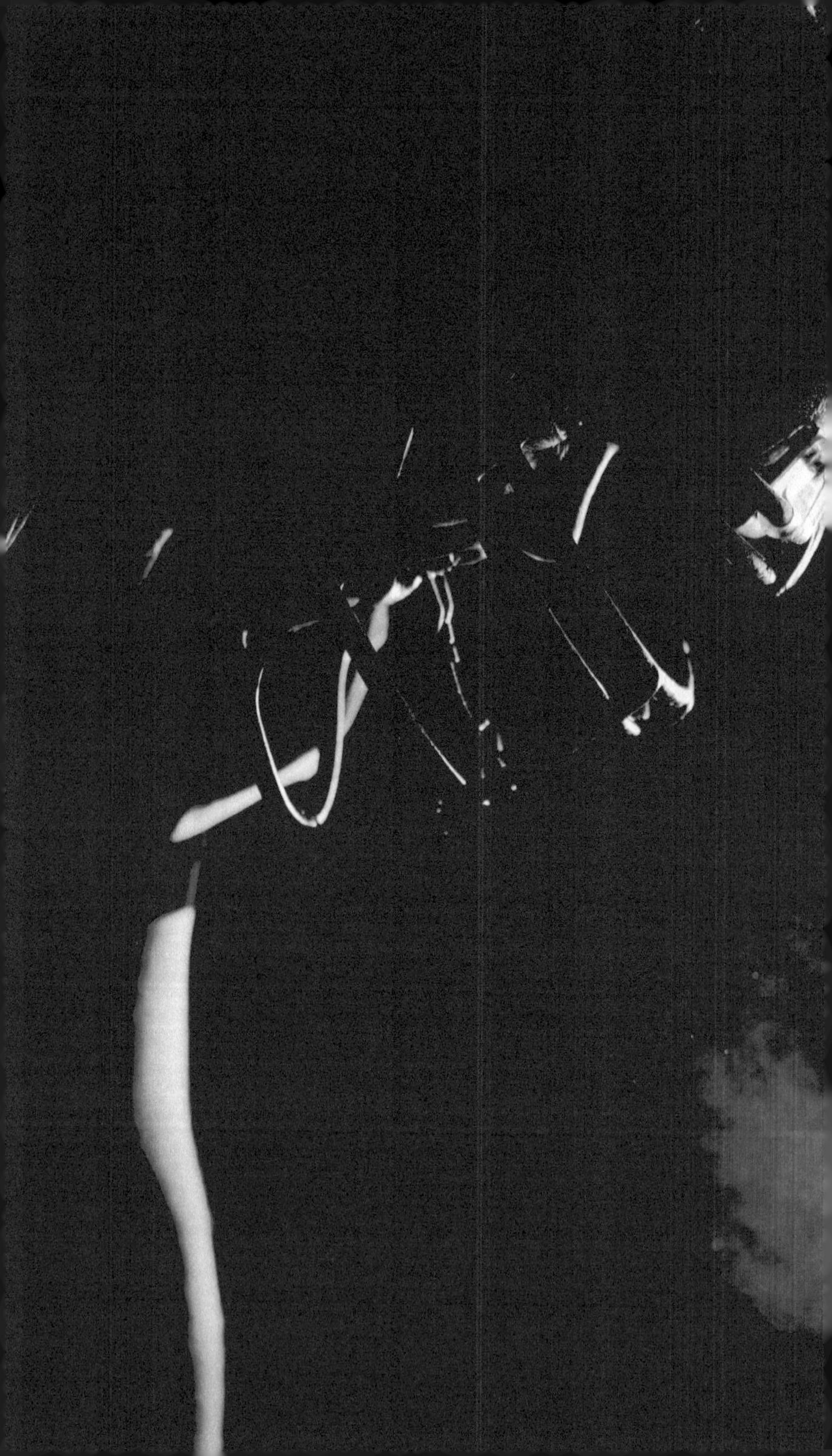

# Chapter Four

## LOGAN

"Audrey?"

My heart is pounding against my rib cage. I'd know that laugh anywhere. I used to dream about it on my worst days. About how if she were with me, she'd do everything to make me feel better. To take my mind off the pain in my leg.

"Is that really you?"

Her body stiffens as she turns around.

A million different memories slam into me.

Holy shit.

Audrey Meyers. The first person I ever loved.

She looks the same, but different.

I remember the day I met her like it was yesterday. She was the honorary captain at the Mountain Lions game that day. From the moment I laid eyes on her, I was a goner.

We spent every minute together we could. With my playing schedule and her training, it was hard to see each other.

But whenever we were together, we were so wrapped

up in each other that the outside world just fell away. It was always just the two of us.

Audrey consumed me. The way she gave her heart to me. Loved me. Supported me. She was the best thing to ever happen to me. There was nothing I wouldn't do for her.

Which is why I had to break things off. She went off to Switzerland and I stayed in Denver. Some days I wonder if we really spent all that time together.

My heart gives another painful tug in my chest.

It's the reminder that we really did. That we really loved each other.

And if I'm being honest? The way my heart is clattering around in my chest, that love might still be there.

Tension kicks up around us, a real live, beating thing. One wrong move and it could snap.

"What's with the hair?"

*Jesus, are you a fucking idiot?*

I haven't seen this woman in years and that's one of the first things I ask her?

Instead of shiny blonde locks, her hair is dyed brown. So brown, it's almost black. Her biceps flex as she crosses her arms, pinning me with a stare that should send me running.

Those eyes of hers are the same. Dark brown pools that are sending daggers in my direction.

Shit.

I need to backtrack, and fast.

"What are you doing here?"

"Isn't it obvious?" There's a bite to her tone. Her eyes trail down my body, taking me in.

I forgot what it was like to be under her intense stare. I don't miss the way her gaze lands on my scar. Even after all the surgeries I went through, there's still a gnarly line down my leg.

One that will never go away.

"I'm guessing it's the same reason I'm here."

My voice has her eyes snapping up to meet mine.

This time, she looks chagrined. It's nothing I'm not used to. It's why I wear shorts at the gym and nowhere else. Everyone here is used to it at this point.

But I still hate the looks it draws in town. I never wanted to be the center of attention.

I love playing football. The spotlight that comes with it I could do without. But ever since I got back into town and started rehabbing my leg, it's been all anyone can talk about.

And I fucking hate it with every fiber of my being.

"Logan. Glad you finally decided to grace us with your presence."

Scott interrupts, ignoring the charged air between us.

For a weekday afternoon, it's busy. With the weather changing, more and more people are coming here instead of hiking in the mountains. We're one good snowfall away from this place being packed every day.

"Nowhere else I'd rather be."

Audrey snorts at my words.

Scott's eyes ping-pong back and forth between the two of us.

"You two know each other, I take it?" Scott asks, curiosity getting the best of him.

"No."

"Yes."

We both answer him at the same time.

"Right." He draws the word out, clearly not believing either one of us. "I'm going to assume you do and also assume it's something I don't want to get in the middle of."

Audrey turns her glare to Scott.

"Why don't you two hit the treadmills? Normal splits to warm up. I need to go do…something." He bolts away from us like a scared kitten.

"Fuck," Audrey whispers to herself.

"Do you, uh, know where the treadmills are?"

"Yes, Logan. I have eyes."

She spins, looking around the gym as if trying to find them. When the hell did she get here?

Holy shit. I should not be getting hard at the way she spits out my name. But it reminds me of the times we used to fight.

Nothing major. Normal couple things. But enough that whenever she said my name—*Logan*, just Logan—I had to have her. We'd combust.

Fuck, if it wasn't one of the best things about being with her.

I follow after her as she goes to the area of the gym where the treadmills are. I can see the scar on the side of her knee from here.

It's small. I still remember seeing her crash. She'd had a few here and there over the years. It's expected in down-hill skiing. How do you learn what not to do if you don't do it is what Audrey always told me.

But when I saw her crash that fateful day, I knew it was different from the others. She didn't bounce back up. She wasn't griping about an icy spot on the moguls near the gate after disqualifying.

My heart was in my throat the entire time I was watching it unfold. I wanted to call her so many times. I knew what she was going through. I was in the thick of my recovery when it happened, so I had nothing but time on my hands.

Hell, I had to give my brother my phone so I wouldn't be tempted.

Why would she have wanted to hear from me?

Audrey punches the buttons on the treadmill with more force than necessary. It shouldn't give me this much joy to see her so riled up.

But why else would she be this rattled if seeing me isn't causing a reaction in her?

I pretend to wipe the sweat from my face to hide my smile.

I was never good at keeping my reactions to myself. Gramps says I always wear my heart on my sleeve.

Setting my speed to my usual starting pace, something slow to ease myself into it, I can't help but keep peering at Audrey.

Her pace matches mine until I see her eyes drift over to me. She ticks her speed up another notch. Fine. If that's how she wants to play it, two can play at that game.

I tick my speed up two higher. This was always one of the things I loved most about Audrey. Her competitive spirit.

Every time we played a game, we'd up the stakes. Something had to be on the line. We loved outdoing one another —seeing who could make the other do something ridiculous.

It usually ended up with some pretty hot sex too.

Shit. I really need to stop thinking about her in bed. It's only going to make this situation more awkward.

Audrey one-ups me again and I follow.

*So much for starting out slow.*

The faster I go, the more I can feel the pinch in my leg. I shouldn't keep pressing, but it's not an unwelcome feeling. It's like my body is finally at the point where I can push it, and I don't have to worry about falling down.

The top of the mountain of my recovery is in sight, and I'm ready to stake the flag that I'm done.

My feet are pounding the tread. Music thumps overhead as I focus on the run…and on Audrey next to me. We're pushing ourselves to the max. If I am, I know she is. Neither one of us want to admit defeat.

"Would you two fucking knock it off?" Scott bellows, standing entirely too close to us. "I don't need you two getting hurt because you're trying to outdo each other. This isn't a pissing contest."

"We are not!" we both tell him at the same time.

Audrey turns to look at me, a smile on her face that's quickly wiped away when she remembers it's me.

"I don't give a shit. Cut it out." Scott goes back to helping someone else on their machine.

"It's your fault." Audrey stops her machine and grabs a towel to wipe her face. I come to a stop, hopping off and placing my feet on the sides of the treadmill.

"My fault? You started it."

She rolls her eyes at me. "Real mature, Logan. And here I thought you were a grown-up."

"Ouch. You were the one who just had to go faster."

"Maybe it's because I'm a better runner than you."

Audrey crosses her arms, stepping into my space. She's a full head shorter than I am, but with the way she's staring up at me, you wouldn't know it.

"Doubt it. I had the fastest hundred-yard dash time as a rookie."

"Easy to run fast when three hundred-pound linebackers are chasing you down, Logan."

"There's an easy way to settle this." I dip my head ever so closer to her.

There's a spark in her eyes. It would be easy to miss if you didn't know her. But even though I haven't seen

Audrey in years, I still know her. Every subtle move she makes I'm in tune with.

"You sure you want to get beat that badly, Winchester?"

The silky smoothness of her voice washes over me and fits into every broken piece of me.

Fuck. I want to go toe to toe with her. Audrey never backs down from a challenge. Another thing that takes me back to when I was in love with…

Love?

I shake my head. *That's a dangerous road to be going down.*

"Am I going to have to separate you two?" Scott sounds like an exasperated parent trying to keep his kids from fighting. "Logan, you're done for the day. Go home. Audrey, hit the weights."

Scott startles me, causing me to trip and fall over the treadmill.

"See? Exactly what I don't want to happen."

"I'm fine." I pop up on both feet easily.

"Then take your fine ass home," Scott bemoans.

"Aww, I knew you liked me." I give his shoulder a playful punch.

"We'll see how much you like me tomorrow."

"Love you too, bro," I call after his retreating form.

Audrey's already marching off behind him to the free weights.

"Audrey."

"What?" Her voice is edgy, like she's already accepted the fact that I'm here and she can't wish me away.

"It's good to see you."

I leave it at that, turning to head home. Back to Dixon.

Even though there's nothing I want more than to turn around and see her. Drink her in. Let my eyes have their fill of her. It's been too damn long since I've seen her. Since I've felt anything real.

Sure, I dated a few women after her. But no one ever compared. Audrey was the bar that no one ever came close to reaching.

It's surreal that she's here.

Audrey is in Jackson.

My Audrey.

When I left her, I never thought I'd see her again. That was it. We were over. Done. Nothing more was to ever come of our relationship.

Maybe it's not just a second chance to regain my football career.

Maybe it's a second chance for the two of us.

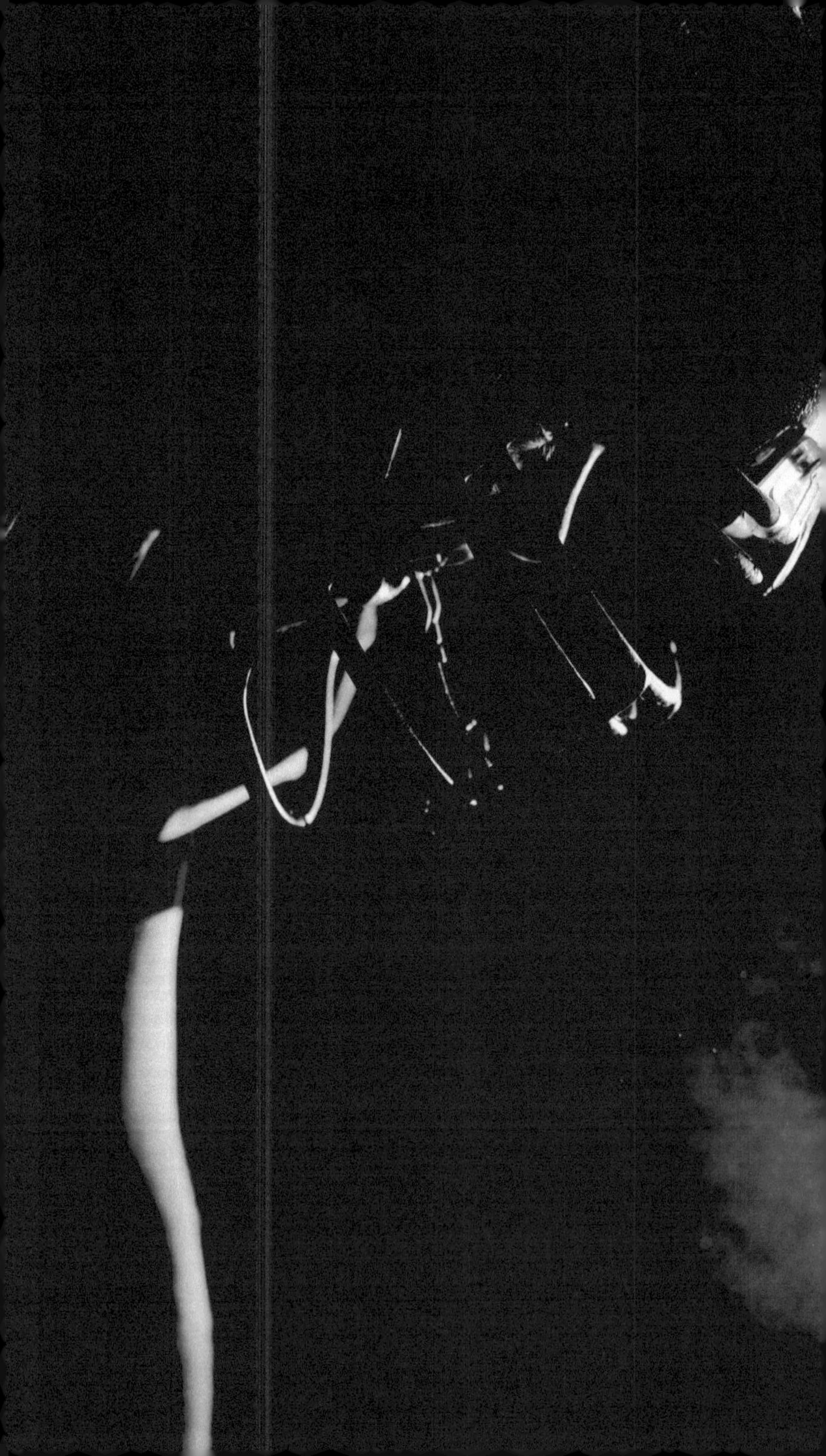

# Chapter Five

## LOGAN

"You're looking really good, Logan."

"Thanks, Heather."

"Now give me ten more."

I laugh. "I should've known it wouldn't be that easy. You're worse than Scott."

I hate squat presses, but I know they're good for me. Centering my focus, I power through the last set of the day.

Rehab hasn't been easy, but these last few weeks I'm finally—*fucking finally*—feeling like myself again. Like I'm the football player I used to be.

"I'm really proud of you, Logan. The progress you've made is incredible." She wraps me in a quick hug after I'm done. Heather and Scott have become like family to me. Being that I practically live here, it's hard not to feel that way.

Turning toward the water cooler, a set of glaring brown eyes meet mine.

Audrey.

"What are you looking at?"

The furrow between her brow only gets deeper. "Nothing. Why are you assuming I'm looking at you?"

Just like Audrey. Never wanting to be caught doing something she isn't supposed to be doing.

"Well, you were."

"Was not."

I step closer to her. Sweat lines her forehead from her own workout. It reminds me of all the things we used to do that would get both of us sweaty.

Shit. These are not thoughts I should be thinking about Audrey. Not when she's now glaring at me.

"Whatever, Logan." She turns, trying to brush me off. "I need to get back to my workout."

"And I've got to get going. Family dinner." I pull my hoodie down over my head.

This time, when Audrey faces me, a warm smile tips her mouth up. "How is your family? I always liked them."

"Good. Hovering over me too much, but good. You can always join me."

"No." Her answer is immediate.

"Invite stands. If you ever want a home-cooked meal, I know they would love to see you."

"Thanks, but I need to finish here today."

"I'll see you tomorrow."

Audrey ignores my goodbye as she goes back to the weight bench. Not that I can blame her.

She consumes my every thought as I head back to Dixon for the night.

The thought of Audrey coming to family dinner would almost be too much for me right now. The few times Audrey came home to Dixon with me, my entire family loved her. It's not that they're a hard bunch to get to know, but they're protective.

I still remember how upset they were when I told them

Audrey and I had broken up. The details I gave them were sparse. I knew they'd be pissed at me.

Hell, I was pissed at me. But I did it for the right reasons.

Maybe one of these days Audrey will stop looking at me like I'm the gum under her shoe.

By the time I'm pulling in to the ranch, darkness has settled across the mountains.

I love this time of year. Something about winter coming and the coldness it brings always settles me. It was always one of my favorite times to play football. Who wouldn't want to play in the snow?

I only hope that I get to do it again one day.

Based on the number of cars, I'm the last one here.

"There's my favorite grandson." Gramps pulls me in for a hug as soon as I walk in the door. The open room is packed to the brim. People on couches. Others setting the table. It's almost too small to fit all of us, but it's cozy. Where we'd always come growing up even though we lived close by.

It's everything a grandparents' house should be.

"That's just mean," Peter says. "I thought I was the favorite."

"You can be the favorite tomorrow when you remember to bring more Claras over for me."

"Suck it, bro." I give him a playful punch as I toe out of my tennis shoes. "What's for dinner?"

"Chef Wayne is trying out some new recipes over at the ranch, so we get the extras." Gemma sets a huge platter of chicken down. "It's a new lemon cream sauce."

It smells and looks delicious. One of the perks of owning the ranch is we get all the food they test out. Baked potatoes, macaroni, rolls, and steaming Brussels sprouts sit on the dining room table. With the way the Winchester clan has been growing these last few years, there's not much room left for us to sit.

"You want something to drink?" Nash asks as I amble over to the table.

"I'll take whatever beer we have."

"You got it."

It's weird not seeing Peter and Nash as much anymore. Once I was able to start driving myself to rehab, I moved out of their place. I don't know if I would have made it through those first few months if I weren't living with them.

"How was rehab today?"

"It was a bitch."

I grab the beer from Nash as he takes a seat next to Peter. Looking around, I'm reminded I'm the only one here that's not partnered.

Don't get me wrong, I love my siblings and their partners. But sometimes, the fact that I'm alone is glaringly obvious.

Not that bringing Audrey here tonight was the solution. But fuck, do I ever miss her at times like this. She fit in so well with my family. Never one to take shit from them and always gave as good as she got.

"When do you get to play football again, Uncle Logan?" Willow asks from across the table, scooping over half the macaroni onto her plate.

"Not sure." Out of everyone here, Willow is probably my biggest fan.

"Do you know when you'll be meeting with the team?" Mason asks, putting half of the noodles that Willow put on her plate back in the bowl. It's hard not to laugh at the mean mug she's giving him.

I shake my head, grabbing my beer and taking a long pull. "Not yet."

What I don't tell my brother is that I've been avoiding their calls. Back when I was still having regular surgeries, my doctors would keep the team docs updated. After that, they left it up to me. A few calls here and there. But now that the time to face them is bearing down on me, it's getting hard to pick up. There's something in my gut that has me worried.

What if I'm doing all this work and it's for nothing? What if my leg isn't strong enough? What if I'm done with football?

I've been to hell and back these last couple of years. I wouldn't wish what I've been through on my worst enemy. But the nagging thought has taken hold in the back of my head and I can't seem to get past it. No matter how much I want my future in football back.

*What if it's not enough?*

"You'd think they'd want their best running back on the field again." Gemma's voice is defensive on my behalf.

"I don't like that Rodgers guy," Willow pipes up. "He fumbles too much."

"I agree, Pipsqueak." The guy is good, but he loses the ball too much.

"I'm not a Pipsqueak anymore!"

"Sorry." I throw my hands up in defense. "I forgot."

"Welcome to my world," Mason mumbles.

"What did we say about yelling at people about that?" Ivy's voice is calm, as she reaches out to smooth Willow's wild curls.

Willow puffs out a breath, like this isn't the first time she's been told this. "That the people who call me Pipsqueak love me and I shouldn't be mad that they love me."

"That's right." She drops a kiss on her head. "Now, pass me the mac and cheese."

"Other than the team ghosting you, how was training today? Heather not being too hard on you?" Mason asks.

I love how involved my family is in my recovery.

"Nah. It's not her I need to worry about. Audrey's been busting my balls."

"Busting your balls?" Willow asks. "What's that?"

I look up from my plate and realize then what I said. Every set of eyes is focused on me before the room explodes into chaos.

"Wait, Audrey's back?"

"What's she doing here?"

"Why didn't you tell us she was back?"

"When did she get here?"

"Holy shit."

"Wait, who's Audrey?" Blake's voice cuts through the noise.

"Only the love of his life," Gemma clarifies for him.

"Was. Was the love of my life," I correct her.

"Then why are you blushing?" Gemma points her fork at me.

"I am not."

At least, I don't think I am.

God, I forgot how invasive my siblings can be when they're grilling someone on their love life. They show no mercy.

"Why didn't you tell us she was back?" Nash asks. "This is big."

"Bigger than big. This is huge!" Gemma's voice is loud.

"Okay, it's not that big," I correct her.

"I wasn't around much when you brought her home before," Ivy starts, "but even I know what she meant to you."

"Jesus. You guys have the biggest mouths."

I shake my head, popping a crispy Brussels sprout in my mouth, giving me a minute to collect my thoughts.

*Shit, that's good.*

The last thing I wanted to do was tell my family Audrey was back. For this reason. I was already freaking out over it, and I didn't need them to freak out too.

Audrey is here for the exact same reason I am. Training and rehab. Both of us have goals and are trying to get back to peak physical shape.

We're like two ships passing in the night. Only here with each other for a little while. Then she's off to competitions all over the world, and I'm hopefully back to Denver.

"She's only here for a few weeks. It's not a big deal."

"You're so full of shit." Mason is laughing at me now. "You don't want to admit what she still means to you."

Fucking older brothers.

"Meant. Past tense." I grab the roll off my plate and chuck it at his head. Mason plucks it out of the air and tosses it right back at me. My dodge is skillful as it bounces along the floor and lands at Daisy's paws. She happily eats it up.

"No throwing food at the dinner table." Gramps's voice quiets everyone.

"Hey! I want to throw food!" Willow whines. "Why do adults get to do everything?"

"Because we're adults, Willow. I promise you, one day you'll get to throw a roll at Uncle Logan's head."

"Yes!" She goes back to eating her mac and cheese with a happy smile on her face.

"Logan, can we talk outside?" Gramps asks, standing from his chair.

I don't miss the way everyone tracks us as we head out the door.

"So, Audrey is back." Gramps leans back in his rocker. It creaks on the old wooden boards. I stare out at the bare trees in the front yard as I kick my feet up on the railing.

"She is."

"How do you feel about that?" Gramps sips on his scotch.

"Honestly? I don't know."

It's hard to voice the thoughts racing through my head.

"You loved her. You have to have some feelings on her coming back."

I wish I had a drink right now. Anything to distract myself from thoughts of Audrey.

Since the minute she walked into the gym, she's consumed my every waking thought. It's been years since I last saw her, but even then, she's always been with me.

I watched every single one of her races. Cheered her on and felt her heartache when she lost. There has never been another person who has had such a hold over me.

Only Audrey.

"I've missed her, Gramps. But she really doesn't want anything to do with me."

"Does she know why you let her go?"

"No."

The only person who knows the real reason is sitting next to me. When Gramps asked about her, I couldn't lie. But I also didn't want my entire family to know. I hated how I ended things with her. A coward's way out.

But she deserved everything that she's gotten since I left her. A few World Cup medals and new sponsorships. She's out there taking over while my life came to a grinding halt.

"You need to tell her, son. She deserves the truth."

"And what if she hates me even more because of it?"

"Then that's a risk you'll have to take."

I know Gramps is right. Audrey needs to know why I

let her go. Not because I didn't love her, but because I didn't want her to stay behind because of me.

What if she forgives me? What if this could be a second chance for the two of us?

I'm afraid to even entertain the idea. Audrey was the best thing to ever happen to me. Do I want a second chance with her? Of course I do. But I don't even have any idea what her current relationship status is, so it might be too much to hope for.

Maybe she was sent here for a reason. Maybe it's our chance.

Maybe…just, maybe this is a risk I want to take.

Because it could give me back everything I've always wanted.

My career *and* Audrey.

# Chapter Six



A biting cold wind whips through the town.

Fuck. I don't remember it being this cold here.

With getting a place in town near the gym, I don't bother with my car. The one thing I do remember about this place? Everything is a five-minute walk away.

And the more I'm out and about on my leg, the better off I'll be.

Except, fuck, it's freezing today.

The sooner I can get to the gym, the sooner I can be home and not around the man who is now consuming my every thought.

What are the odds that I would run into Logan?

Pushing open the door to the gym, I'm met with a wall of heat.

I'm ready to work this man out of my system. Nothing helps my busy mind more than getting lost in a workout.

"Audrey, hey." Scott greets me as I shrug out of my coat. "How are you adjusting to Jackson?"

"Good. Although, I'm pretty sure a moose woke me up at two in the morning?"

Scott laughs. "Are you by chance staying by the Screaming Moose?"

I wince. "That rings a bell."

"One of Jackson's most notorious hotspots. The moose on top of the bar screams sometimes. No one can figure out how to change it, so it starts screaming whenever it wants. A town legend if you will."

"Are you talking about Mike?"

Urgh. I wish that voice didn't sound like nails on a chalkboard to me right now. Except it does.

Logan.

His smile is bright as he inserts himself in our conversation.

"Audrey is staying near the Screaming Moose."

"Whose name is apparently Mike," I grumble.

"You'll learn to love him," Logan tells me, eyes trained on me. "We all do."

He holds my gaze. As if telling me I'll learn to love him again.

Fat chance of that happening.

Not when he ripped my heart out and stomped all over it.

"What's the plan for today, Scott?" I ask, shaking off Logan's stare. If I'm going to be here with him the next few weeks, I need to put him in my rearview mirror. Shrug him off like I did my coat and do what I came to do.

"Today is leg day for you." The sadist that he is grins at me.

I groan. "My favorite."

"And when you win your next medal, you can thank me in your victory speech."

"I'll be sure to do that."

Scott walks me through my workout for the day. Nothing that I haven't already been doing at home.

Moving off to my own mat, far away from Logan, I run through my drills. The gym fills up around me as the day moves on.

The more work I do, the more squats I sink into, the easier it is to quiet the storm of emotions inside of me.

My presence here goes unnoticed. It could be because of Scott's notoriety, but it seems famous athletes are the norm around here.

This is exactly what I needed. To get out of the chaos in Copper Mountain and be somewhere not in the thick of the team's training.

It's easy to get wrapped up in the drama of who's sleeping with whom. Here? I can come to the gym, get in some runs on the nearby slopes, and head back to my tiny place. All by myself.

It's perfect.

Between rounds, I hit the treadmill. My pace is easier than it was the first day I was here. No one to compete with or get in my head. Just the pumping of my muscles and my feet pounding the tread.

Yet, no matter what I seem to do, I feel eyes on me. It doesn't take a rocket scientist to figure out who.

Logan.

Wherever I am in the gym, his gaze is tracking me. It sends prickles down my back.

I don't want to be affected by this man.

I thought what happened between us was in the past.

But as I move to the mats to start my next set, Logan is scrambling my brain.

My next set starts with one-leg weighted squats. It's great for my balance, but now my concentration is shot. With Logan so close, only a mat away, it's hard to ignore his presence.

I bend down, touching the weights to the floor, and push back up, staying on one leg.

"You're not doing it right."

I grimace as Logan gives advice from where he's lying on the ground doing push-ups.

"Yes I am."

"Your form is off."

I take a deep breath, focusing on exactly that, and push his voice out of my head.

"My form is fine."

"Let me help." Logan pops up beside me.

"I'm fine. I don't need your help." I try to shake him off. He's like a gnat that won't go away.

"You're leaning forward too much and not sinking back." He tries to grab the weights from me.

"I said I'm fine."

"If you do it like this—"

"I don't need your help!" The facade snaps. I let my anger get the best of me. My eyes dart around the gym. It seems like everyone is staring at us.

Damn it. All I wanted was to come here, lie low, and finish rehab. I didn't want eyes on me. I wanted to stay out of the limelight.

Not run into Logan and get in fights with him over technique.

"I'm fine." I grind my teeth together, pasting on a fake smile. "Leave me alone."

"Fine," Logan parrots back, stalking off like he's the wronged party.

God. Why does that make *me* feel bad? It adds that much more fuel to my fire. I can do this. And do it without him. I've been at it for three years without him.

I don't need him.

I didn't then. And I don't now.

If this is how the next few weeks are going to be, I would've been better off staying in Copper Mountain.

Fucking ex-boyfriend fucking with my head.

So much for a peaceful few weeks away.

# Chapter Seven

AUDREY

"Two more sets, Audrey, and then I want you to stretch before hitting the treadmill."

"Got it, Scott."

"Don't push yourself too hard," Scott warns me. "You athletes don't know your own limits sometimes."

"I'm okay."

I dig into the skater lunges, moving and twisting my body. I don't know how, but in the short time I've been here, I already feel stronger, if that's possible. This is exactly what I needed.

Scott is one of the best, and it's like he knows what we need to do without us knowing it. Trainers like him don't come along often, so I want to take advantage while I can.

These two weeks since I arrived have flown by. I'm getting stronger and stronger. My life revolves around this place and the nearby ski slopes. Because with any hope, I'll be out of here in a few weeks and off to my qualifiers.

Except on the next rep, when my knee bends, something feels wrong and I drop to the mat.

"Damn it." I pound my fist into the mat.

"Are you okay?" Scott appears before me. It seems no matter where he is in the gym, he's always right there when you need him.

"It hurts." I wince as Scott moves my leg.

"Did anything pop?"

I shake my head.

"Just a pull, I think." I press the heels of my hands into my eyes. Shit, this is not what I needed.

"I can take you into town for an X-ray if you think you need it, but is it possible you just overdid it?"

"I don't need one."

The last thing I need is this getting back my coach and him scaling back my workouts. I reach for his hand, standing up. There's a bit of pressure, but nothing that I can't live with.

Thank God.

If I couldn't put any weight on it, it'd be the worst possible scenario. I have the next few months mapped out —almost down to the minute.

And a setback is not in my plans.

"I want you to take the next few days off and rest it. And I mean it. We won't let you in here if you try to come. This is what I mean about knowing your limits."

"I wasn't doing anything hard."

Unlike some people, I actually listen to my trainers. I want to get healthy and back to peak shape as much as the next person.

He raises a brow in my direction, folding his beefy arms across his chest.

"I'm serious!" I balk. "I'm not like…Logan and don't listen."

"Who's saying I don't listen?"

"Audrey's calling you out, man." Scott looks giddy. It's almost like he knows there's tension between the two of us.

My guess is Heather has filled him in. Men aren't that observant.

"I take offense to that. I listen."

"Do you?" I cross my arms at him, mirroring Scott's stance.

"Why do I feel like I'm in trouble and I didn't do anything for once?"

I point a finger at him. "The for once is the problem there."

"Hey!" He throws his hands up in defense. "I was doing just fine minding my own business with my own damn workout."

"I'm not getting in the middle of this." Scott turns to leave. "Audrey, I'll see you back here Monday and not a minute before. Take care of that leg."

"What happened?" Logan's eyes dart to mine.

I walk over to the lockers, mindful of said leg. It hurts, but nothing that I haven't dealt with before.

"Just overdid it."

"Mind if I take a look?"

Logan's face is soft, like he really does want to help me. I don't want to have to rely on him. I don't want to show him any weakness.

Considering how long he's been rehabbing here, it wouldn't be the worst thing in the world.

"Sure."

Dropping to his knees in front me, he digs his thumbs into the tender muscles by my knee. It takes everything I have not to jump at his touch. But the way he starts moving them?

"That feels good."

"I know." He's not looking at me, concentrating on what he's doing. The cocky smile on his face gives him away. "I know all the tricks."

It feels too good. Having his hands on me like this. It's an innocent touch, but it sends my mind reeling. Heat sizzling in my veins. Closing my eyes, I lean back into the locker for support and let Logan help me.

It's been a long few years without him. Being here with him like this almost makes me forget them.

"Try standing on that." His words break me out of my reverie.

"Wow. That feels a lot better." I take a few steps.

"Told you I know a thing or two." Logan winks and goes to leave.

"How do you do it?" I call him back.

"Do what?"

"Deal with a setback this close to the end."

Logan leans against the lockers. I don't miss the way his biceps flex. He crosses one leg over the other. I really need to stop looking at him like this.

Like I'm thawing to the man that broke my heart.

I don't want to be. It's easier on me to keep up the wall.

He gives me a soft smile. "I make a wish."

"You're still doing that?"

"Why wouldn't I? Never hurts to have a little luck."

It's the one thing Logan and I always did together. No matter where we were in the world, if there was a fountain, we'd make a wish.

A good race. A good game. Another chance to see one another.

It might seem silly, but it was something we always did.

Together.

And the fact that he still does it? My heart is clattering around in my chest.

"Besides,"—brown eyes laser in on mine—"every once in a while, they'll come true."

"Oh yeah?"

"It brought you back, didn't it?"

# Chapter Eight

AUDREY

F inally.

My first day off since I arrived in Jackson. Not that I wanted it to come at the expense of potentially hurting myself, but still. My muscles ache in the best way now. That familiar feeling when I move my body. Even with the small setback, I need a break.

Scott has been pushing me to my limit every day, and with his help, I'll be ready for the events out in Lake Placid in January.

It'll be a tight one to qualify for the games, but not unheard of.

The lightest of snow is falling, making the tiny town of Jackson even more picturesque.

Antler arches over the main square.

The sloped mountains looking postcard-worthy just beyond town.

Shops and restaurants lining the streets.

With ski season underway, it's bustling.

Zipping my coat up, I head to the one restaurant that I never visited before. The Screaming Moose.

An old moose head, decked out with Christmas lights, welcomes me inside. Dark, wood-paneled walls are decorated with more moose heads than I've ever seen in my life. Pictures of Jackson haphazardly hang from the walls. A counter with stools lines one wall while the rest of the diner is buzzing with people.

"Hi there, darlin'. Table for one?" an older woman greets me at the hostess stand.

"Can I order carry-out?"

"Sure thing. Order at the counter when you're ready." She winks at me and hands me a menu that looks bigger than the phonebook.

My eyes grow wider at each flip of the page. I don't think I've ever seen a menu so detailed.

Bison burgers.

Elk burgers.

Cow burgers.

Moose burgers.

*Is there such a thing as moose burgers?*

I don't want to order and find out.

"Audrey? Is that you?"

My name being called pulls my attention away from the menu.

"Gemma."

Logan's little sister.

"I thought that was you." She gets up from her table and comes over to wrap me in a hug. "It's so good to see you. Logan said you were in town."

I fight the grimace on my face. Because of course my arrival in town is news for the Winchester family.

As much as I hate it now, it was one of the things I loved most about Logan. His big, loud, and crazy family.

"Only here for a few weeks. Finishing up rehab."

Her eyes glance down to my leg. "Logan said you were injured."

I wave her off. "I'll be back in shape in no time."

"Are you meeting anyone?"

I shake my head, holding the menu in front of me like a shield. I can only guess at what's coming next. "Just grabbing something to go."

"You have to join us."

"That's okay. I don't want to intrude."

Grabbing the menu from my arms, she sets it on the hostess stand and pulls me after her. "I'm not taking no for an answer."

Nerves swell in my belly as Gemma stops at a table with two others.

"Ivy. Look who's here. This is Audrey."

"Audrey?" She eyes me. "The Audrey?"

She tries to whisper, but it doesn't come out that way.

"Who's Audrey?" the little girl next to her asks, looking up from her book.

"Sorry. Where are my manners? I'm Ivy, Mason's fiancée."

"Nice to meet you." I take her proffered hand.

"And this is my future stepdaughter, Willow."

The girl with curly hair looks up and smiles at me.

I remember her. Logan was such a proud uncle. Still is. "The number one Mountain Lions fan."

She pins me with a fierce stare. It reminds me of Logan. "How do you know that?"

"Your Uncle Logan talked about you all the time."

"I don't remember you."

"You were a baby when I first met you."

She shrugs a shoulder and goes back to her book.

"I invited Audrey to join us."

"Really. It's okay. I was just going to grab and go."

"Nonsense." Ivy shakes her head. "The Screaming Moose is best appreciated in the restaurant. We'd really love for you to join us."

Gemma pushes the seat next to her out. "We don't bite. Promise."

"I'll be the judge of that." I laugh, dropping into the seat. Their warm smiles do a lot to quell the roiling nerves in my belly.

Logan always loved his family. Hell, I did too. Being an only child, I lived for the Winchester family dinners whenever we came to visit. Gramps was always one of the most kind and welcoming people to me. I never felt like an outsider.

"So you're back in Jackson?" Gemma rests her chin in her hand, leaning toward me. A diamond engagement ring glints off the lights.

"I am. It looks like you got engaged."

This puts a winning smile on her face. "Got married over the summer."

"Wow. Seems like you Winchesters are all pairing off."

I guess not Logan, though. But I can't think about that right now. Logan isn't mine. I was his to forget. To cast aside and move on from like we meant nothing.

Now is not the time to have those thoughts plague me.

"Can I go play on the pinball machine? This is boring." Willow sets her book down.

Ivy digs around in her purse and hands her some change. "Have at it."

Willow gives her a hug before dashing off.

"She's a cute kid."

"She's the best." Ivy watches her as she pops a quarter in the machine and starts playing.

A waitress comes and take our order.

"Grilled chicken salad? Not feeling adventurous?" Ivy asks me.

"I was worried what I would get with a moose burger on the menu."

Gemma laughs. "It's not real moose. The bun is grilled with a moose face in it."

"Thank God." I fiddle with the napkin ring in front of me. "I don't think I could look at a moose the same way if I ate one of them."

"Are you getting out while you're here?" Ivy asks, sipping on her water.

"More or less. Main concern is rehab."

"You sound just like Logan. Rehab has been his only focus for the last year."

"A year? How bad was his injury?"

"You don't know?" Gemma asks.

"Gemma," Ivy hisses. "It's not like they were together."

"He was lost without you," Gemma goes on, ignoring Ivy.

"What?" This woman is going to give me whiplash at how fast she's changing topics. "He dumped me."

"Just because you're not with someone, doesn't mean you don't still love them."

"Could we please not talk about this?"

An awkward silence settles over the table. Thankfully, the waitress chooses that moment to drop off our food. I don't think I've ever been happier to see a salad in my life.

"Willow. Lunch is here."

She skips her way back over to the table and happily digs into her chicken fingers.

*Sorry*, Gemma mouths to me. I give her a smile, letting her know not to worry about it.

That'll be me for the next few weeks. Churning over everything she just told me. Whether she meant to or not.

The rest of lunch is easy conversation, mostly Willow chatting about anything that comes to mind. It's a nice distraction from Gemma's words.

Logan was lost? He's the one that broke my heart. He doesn't get to act like the victim in all of this. But something else Gemma said is ringing louder.

Logan's been in rehab for a year? Sure, I knew he hurt himself, but is this the same injury? I made it a point not to search out information about him. And if it is from that same injury in the Super Bowl, what happened that made him wait so long to start rehab?

When I say goodbye to Gemma, Ivy, and Willow, all I'm left feeling is confused.

I told myself I'd be okay not speaking to Logan at the gym after seeing him for the first time. Am I still okay with that? I don't know, but Gemma's words make me want to dig a little deeper. Figure out what's going on with him.

The Logan I knew never had a care in the world. The one I saw for the first time in years is the same way.

What if it's all a facade? What if there's more going on?

So much for burying my head in the sand and ignoring the man. Because all I want to do now is ask him these questions.

Serves me right for coming to the Screaming Moose.

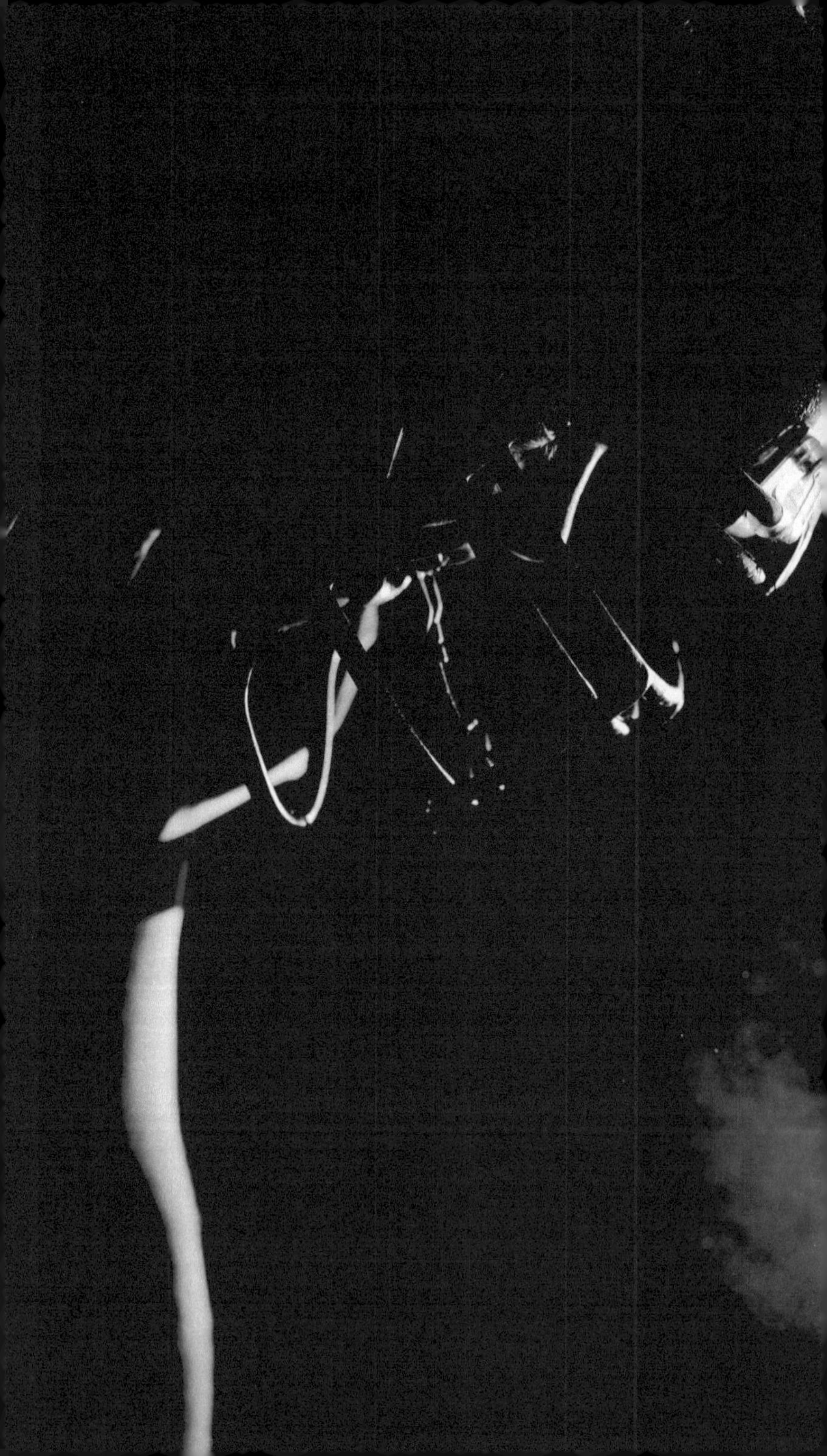

# Chapter Nine

LOGAN

"Have you given any thought as to when you'll take your physical?"

I eye Scott from my spot on the mat. I got here early, needing to work myself hard. Things with Audrey have been…weird.

It's like one minute she hates me and the next she's looking at me like she wants to be my friend.

It's fucking with my head.

And no better way to clear it *the upstairs one* than with a hard workout.

"Ready to get rid of me?"

Sitting up, I wipe the sweat from my brow. Even though the garage doors are open letting in the cool air, it's hot in here.

"You're more than ready. What's keeping you here?"

"I've got my reasons."

All five feet, nine inches with dark hair, a beautiful smile, and a look that could kill me. But I don't tell him that.

"Don't let fear hold you back. You were one of the best

running backs when you were playing. I'd hate to see you get in your head about this."

"You're starting to sound like Willow."

Scott huffs. "She's got a point. Rodgers fumbles too much."

"No need to rush things. I just want a few more weeks."

I want to be in peak physical shape. It's not that staying here is going to hurt me at all. Besides, this late in the season, it's unlikely I'll play anyway.

At least that's what I keep telling myself.

I'm not ready to meet my fate just yet.

"Just don't fuck it up this close to the finish, alright?"

"What, me? Never." I chuck my dirty towel at him.

"I'll be glad to be done with you, Winchester." His words hold no malice.

"It's like you really do love me."

Scott points at me, an idea coming to mind. "And just for that, you and Audrey are going to do the trail run today."

"I take it all back," I whine.

I fucking hate the trail run.

"Too late." He turns, finding Audrey on the leg machine and calling her over.

"What's up, Scott?"

Her dark hair is twisted up in a braid around her head. It's still weird to see her like this. Not a blonde hair in sight.

"You and Logan are hitting the trails today. Two-mile loop and back."

"What the hell? I thought we only had to do it once a week?"

His smile is cunning. "Too bad. You're doing it with him."

"This is his doing, isn't it?" She thumbs in my direction.

"It usually is."

"I'm standing right here, you know."

They ignore me. "First one back gets to go home when they get back."

"Don't have to tell me twice." Audrey sprints off through the open gym door.

"You fucker!" I yell at him as I chase after Audrey.

Something I'm familiar with.

Having no time to prepare, I focus on my goal. Catching the woman in front of me.

With the gym's location on the edge of Jackson, we back up to the foothills, where there isn't any snow on the ground yet. Which means there is the perfect running trail, the first part mostly uphill, that Scott fucking loves making us run.

Says it builds character.

I think he just likes seeing us in pain.

*What an asshole.*

I close the distance easily with Audrey and try to slow her down to a more reasonable pace.

"Leg's feeling better?"

She doesn't look at me, keeping her vision laser-focused on the trail ahead.

"Much."

"Did you ice it?"

"Yes."

"Wow. What a conversationalist you are."

This draws her to an immediate stop.

"We don't have to have some big heart-to-heart. Casual is okay."

Ouch. Okay.

"Sorry, I guess I'll keep my mouth shut."

I push past her, cutting her off at the fork in the trail.

"You don't need to pout about it."

"I'm not." I totally am. It'd put Willow to shame. "I'm just trying to respect your wishes."

"Logan, stop."

Dark clouds have been moving in all day. With how cold it's been, it seems the first big snowfall in town will be here at any moment.

"Look, I'm sorry. If you don't want to talk, we can do this run and be done. I'll even let you win so you don't have to hang out with me at the gym."

Her brows pull together, breath leaving her chest in big puffs.

"Did you ever think about how hard this is for me?"

"What?"

"Logan, I loved you and out of the blue you ended this. I was devastated. Did you stop to think that maybe, *just maybe*, being here and being around you is hard for me?"

I kick a rock in the dirt. "Of course I've thought about it."

"I've come to terms with the fact that you're here. Fine. I knew it was a possibility. I'm just trying to get through this with my heart in one piece."

This really isn't the time to have it out. But she's right. It's not fair to her to keep trying to get her attention when she wants nothing to do with me.

"Okay."

"Okay?" She sounds confused. "You're giving me what I want that easily?"

"If it's what you want, I won't bother you. I'm not going to fight you on it."

No matter how much I want to be near her, I have to respect her wishes.

"Just…maybe don't be around all the time?"

"Some of it?"

She smiles at me as she takes off up the trail. "Some of it is fine."

I let her go this time, giving her what she wants. Yet, at the same time, it's the smallest sliver of hope. What I told Scott was true.

If the team called me today and needed me to try out again, I'd be ready. Except Audrey is here now. This is a chance I didn't think I would get again.

I can't leave. Not now. The love of my life was sent here for a reason. I'd be stupid to turn away from that.

As the wind picks up again, my pace starts to slow. Audrey is still a ways ahead of me, but I don't mind. It's a view I enjoy. She's always had a great ass.

The drop-off starts, and it helps me close the distance between us.

"I'm coming for you, Meyers!" I yell at her.

"In your dreams, Winchester!" her voice carries back to me.

With the gym in sight, I push forward with all I have, but it's not enough.

"First!" Audrey drops her hands to her knees, taking in gulping breaths. "Suck it, Winchester."

I quirk a brow in her direction. "Careful there, I think you might really mean it."

Her face catches up with her words. "I didn't mean it like that."

"Sure you didn't." I hold out my hand to her. "Good race."

Brown eyes assess me, wondering if she can trust me. She takes my hand and a shock of electricity zips through me.

Shit. That hasn't happened in a long time. I half

expect her to drop my hand, but she doesn't. I shake it off the feeling, pulling her close.

"Don't think I'm going to let you win again, Meyers."

The fire in her eyes is back. It's the Audrey I've always known. One who is passionate about competing and can never lose.

The Audrey I fell in love with.

It's nice to see she wasn't hidden in there the whole time.

"Bring it on, Winchester. Bring it on."

She better be ready, because that's exactly what I plan to do.

Catch the woman I let get away.

It's on.

# Chapter Ten



"One more set and then you're done for the day." Scott slaps my leg, urging me to continue.

I towel off the sweat from my forehead, trying to find the energy to keep going. "I hate you. You know that, right?"

"Audrey, if I had a dollar for every time someone said that to me, I wouldn't need to run this place. Now, stop stalling and give me one more set."

"You've got this, Audrey." Logan comes to stand next to Scott, and it sets my teeth on edge.

"I know I do," I snap back.

He throws his hands up and takes a step back. "Sorry."

"He's right. You can do this."

Glaring at both of them, I toss my towel to the ground and sit back on the machine. They're right. I know I can do this, but it doesn't lessen the pressure I'm putting on myself to do ten leg presses.

It's something I used to be able to do in my sleep. It was easy. Now, my legs are screaming at me. I haven't had to work this hard at anything in a long time.

Skiing came easy to me. From the time I strapped on my first pair of skis, I was hooked. I was a student of the sport and learned everything I could until it became second nature.

Now though? After my injury? It's like I have to relearn everything I knew about skiing. I'm not used to being behind the eight ball.

Pressing my legs up for the final time, I bring them back slowly, setting the weight plates down on the stack.

"Hell yeah!" Scott holds his hand out for a fist bump, which I return.

I'm spent. Every muscle in my body hurts. My trainers weren't kidding when they said this guy is good.

Logan gives me a shy smile before walking away.

"He's only trying to help," Scott tells me, watching Logan's retreating form.

"Isn't that your job?" I grab my water bottle, taking a huge gulp.

It feels good working my body like this. An athlete being down with an injury isn't the easiest thing in the world.

"Yes, but Logan's got a knack for this."

"What, being a pain in the ass?" I laugh.

"Helping people. Coaching them. He's good at it."

I track Logan, watching as he goes and does his own workout. Scott's right. It's something Logan excelled at.

It's one of the things I loved most about him.

I don't think he knows how good he is at it. Even if it's driving me crazy.

I'm sure I'm giving him whiplash with how hot and cold I am. I can't help it. I try to let him in, but then my heart catches up with my head and all I'm reminded of is how he hurt me.

Why are relationships so complicated? Not that what we have would be considered a relationship.

Scott leaves me to do some stretches, but it's hard to keep my mind focused. I still can't believe Logan is here. It shouldn't surprise me, seeing as how he lives an hour away from here. But with his injury, I thought the team would have him in Denver under close watch.

I guess his trainers had the same idea that mine did.

With each passing day here, I'm gaining more strength. My leg feels better. Being here has done wonders for my mental health and recovery. Not having to worry about reporters throwing cameras in my face? It would do anyone a world of good.

It figures that the place I'm sent and is good for me also has the one person I never wanted to see again.

"I'll see you tomorrow." Scott waves goodbye as the gym starts to empty out.

"See ya."

Finishing my post-rehab routine, I grab my coat and joggers, getting ready to make the walk back to my place. Pushing open the door, I'm met with the one person I can't seem to shake.

"You did good today," Logan tells me, coming up behind me. "Just wanted to tell you that."

It's dark outside, night blanketing the town early as we head toward winter. This is my favorite time of year. The biting cold of the night air stings my face. There's nothing I love more than curling up in front of the fire with a hot chocolate after a long day on the slopes.

"I don't need your encouragement."

"Sometimes it can help and keep you moving forward."

"I get it, Logan!" It explodes out of me. Every emotion tied to this man has been simmering under the surface and

I can't take it anymore. "I get you want to help, but I don't need it!"

Being this close to the man that broke my heart is messing with my head. He's still that same guy that I met all those years ago at a football game in Denver.

He's also *not* the same guy. So much has changed for him. How can it not with all he must have been through since his injury? But I don't need placating comments about how well I'm doing.

"I'm just trying to help." He's almost sheepish. Why does it make *me* feel bad?

"Scott is doing plenty of that, okay? I don't need you."

"Fine. Do whatever the hell you want, Audrey. I don't care anymore." Logan stalks away from me.

"Oh, now you don't care and are walking away? Again? I guess I should be used to it."

Something sparks behind Logan's brown eyes as he turns back to me. Even in the darkness, I can see it. He's never been one to shy away from showing his emotions.

"You think I wanted to walk away from you?"

"You didn't seem to care. I was yours to forget, Logan. You threw me away."

Logan closes the space between us, but it feels like it's a gulf a mile wide.

"If anything, I cared too much. You think I wanted to see you throw away one of the best opportunities just to stay in Denver with me?"

"What? What in the world are you talking about?"

"The ski school in Switzerland?"

"How did you know about that?"

My mind is spinning. I still remember that fall, when Logan left me. I had the chance to learn from some of the best skiers in the world. It would've been stupid to turn it down. But I was waffling. I was an Olympian. I didn't need to learn more, right? I was fine in Denver.

I had everything I wanted there. Logan. Skiing. I didn't want to rock the boat.

Then Denver had an away game, and I got the call to go and meet with the trainers from Switzerland while they were in town. And that's when Logan told me we were done. Over the phone.

Like the coward that he was. Or so I thought.

"I heard you talking to your mom about it." His voice is quiet. "It was late, so you assumed I was asleep, but I heard everything. I couldn't let you pass up the opportunity of a lifetime for me."

Rage boils inside of me. This is why he left me?

"Don't you think that was a decision I should have gotten to make?" I shove him, but he doesn't move. God, why is this man so infuriating?

"It sounded like a done deal. I wasn't going to be the reason you stayed put. You'd regret it and eventually regret me. I couldn't let that happen."

"You think I don't regret you anyway?" It comes out without my thinking about it.

I take a breath, closing my eyes and trying to find my center. The air shifts around me. Being alone with this man is breaking down every wall I constructed.

"I don't regret my decision." Logan's breath ghosts over my cheek. My body, traitorous as it is, sways into him. "I love you, Audrey. Letting you go was one of the hardest things I ever did. But I couldn't keep you."

"You couldn't keep me? What the hell is that supposed to mean?" Opening my eyes, I see Logan staring down at me.

"I couldn't be the reason you stayed behind. I did what needed to be done. I let you go so you could chase after your dreams. I broke my own damn heart so you would go to Switzerland. I don't regret it—"

"So you've said." I cut him off, a wateriness to my voice that wasn't there before.

"I don't regret it, Audrey, because I saw how well you did there. I watched every competition. Your times got better. You were competing in new races. I knew it was the best thing I could've done for you."

"What you didn't see,"—I straighten, getting right into his face—"was that I spent most nights crying. That I was lonely as hell because no one wanted to hang out with the sad girl who cried all the time. I was heartbroken, Logan. I couldn't figure out why the person I loved most in the world would've left me like that." My voice breaks. "I thought there was someone else."

"God no. There could never have been anyone else. Not with how much I loved you. It nearly broke me, leaving you. If I saw you again, I knew I couldn't go through with it."

"Logan, I…"

"Why didn't you tell me about it? Maybe if you had told me about it, we wouldn't be standing here right now. Maybe things would've been different. But you kept it from me. Why?"

I try to swallow around the lump in my throat. I played out what happened between us so often in my head, I could recite it like my favorite movie.

How did I go from being in love and on top of the world to rock bottom the next day in a foreign country?

I never did tell Logan about Switzerland. Because it meant moving there for training. Not being in the US.

Logan's schedule wouldn't allow him to come visit anytime between August and January. Longer if they made the playoffs. Throw in offseason training and camp? We barely would've seen each other.

Would we have made it through to the other side?

We'll never know.

Snow starts falling from the sky. It's like a sign from the universe that the two of us need to take a minute and breathe.

Logan's warm hand cups my cheek. I draw in a deep breath. It's the first time in years that he's touched me like this.

Familiar.

Intimate.

Loving.

"I will never regret it, Audrey, because I saw you achieve everything you've ever wanted. You were up there living out your dream. Even if it wasn't with me by your side, I was so fucking proud of you."

A lone tear slips through, stinging my cheeks. Logan swipes it away with his thumb.

"I never stopped loving you, Audrey. Call me a masochist, but I always watched your races. I was always cheering you on. I could never let you go. You were my everything."

With a quick kiss to my cheek, Logan is gone. Taking his warmth with him.

Snow falls around me as I watch him leave.

The man that loved me so much, he broke his own heart so I could chase my dream. The man that I've spent the better part of the last few years trying to get over.

Key word—trying.

Because no matter what I did, or who I tried to date, it always came back to him.

To Logan Winchester.

It seems like neither of us let the other one go.

My mind is reeling at his confession.

What if I had told him? Would we still be together? Would we have been there for each other during our darkest days?

The feelings I had toward Logan—anger and hatred—start to slide away. All this time, I thought he didn't care. And why would I when he cast me aside like that?

We were young when we first got together. We got caught up in the emotions of loving someone.

It turns out, I was wrong. Wrong about so many things.

Logan Winchester isn't the man I thought he was.

What if that means I'm here for a reason?

Is there a second chance in our future?

Maybe. Just…maybe.

# Chapter Eleven

## AUDREY

There's nothing like the feeling of flying down the mountain. The swishing of the skis beneath my boots. The snow pelting me in the face.

It's one of the best feelings in the world.

And also helps me clear my head.

Logan's confession the other night has been playing on repeat in my head. I tried to make our relationship ending so abruptly work in my head so many times.

Was it something I did? Did he fall out of love with me? Was there another woman?

Never in my wildest dreams did I think he knew about Switzerland. I kept it so close to the vest, scared how he would take the news. He's a professional football player and I'm a professional skier. Trying to make that work? It would've been too hard.

I didn't know how our relationship would survive it.

But Logan made the decision for us.

Would I trade the time I spent in Switzerland? Not for anything. It made me the skier I am today. I could've done without the abject heartbreak though.

I cruise down the bottom of the hill. The Tetons aren't the hardest mountains to ski, but it's my happy place. These hills are familiar.

Every time Logan brought me here during the winter, we'd go skiing. Logan wasn't the best, opting for caution—no surprise with his career—but I loved the time we got to share together.

Thinking about it now isn't causing that ache in my chest to bloom. Before, anytime I thought about it, it would threaten to split me open. It's why I locked that chapter of my life up into a neat little box.

Now? Now I wish Logan were here with me to ski today.

With the snow coming down in soft waves, it's the perfect day for skiing.

And being that it's the middle of the day, the slopes aren't packed. Groups of kids are learning to ski while others are weaving down the mountain.

Kicking the snow off my skis, I take the lift back to the top.

Cold, deep breaths flood my lungs as I gaze out over the mountain. Deep paths are carved through the snow. Some cut through the pine trees as they all point down to the lodge.

I glide off the lift and head straight into my run.

Form is perfect. Knee feels good. Everything about this run is exactly as it should be.

Being that these runs are easier, even the black diamonds, it lets my mind wander.

What if I was sent here for a reason?

Logan was my everything once upon a time. Even if he couldn't be at every race, I still felt his support. I got to Denver for his games when I could. There was something magical about watching him play. The way he could read a defense and make a cut to get down the field and score was sometimes breathtaking.

Anytime we were apart, we'd video call.

Why would Switzerland have been any different?

Focusing on the past isn't going to help either of us.

But…could this be a second chance for us?

It's been on my mind nonstop since he told me the truth.

With the snow picking up and the cold setting in, I fly to the bottom of the mountain, ready to get inside. I kick off my skis and head toward the lodge.

A wall of heat hits me as I walk in, then run smack into someone. Someone that is built, if the muscles my hands find have anything to say about it.

"Audrey."

It's like my thoughts summoned him here. Of course it'd be Logan.

"Hey." An easy smile curves the corner of his lips.

"Hi." There's a note of shock in my voice. If it weren't for the snow pinkening my cheeks already, my blush would show.

"What are you doing out here?"

"Isn't it obvious?" I return his smile.

"Right." He kicks at something on the ground. This isn't a side of Logan I'm used to.

Strong. Confident. Playful. Loving. Easy to laugh. That's how I would have described Logan to anyone.

Shy? This is something that's new.

"What are you doing out here?"

I pull off my hat, brushing off the snow that's collected there.

"I had to drop off an order from the Tipsy Cocktail."

"Peter's bar, right?" I drop down into one of the chairs

by the fireplace. My legs are gassed after a hard day of runs.

"Yeah. Can I?" He points to the chair opposite me.

"Sure."

"I've been helping out there when I can."

"Football isn't paying the bills anymore?"

He rubs a hand behind his neck. His nervous tell. I hate that I still know these things about him. Logan was never shy about showing me how he felt. He was an open book.

It was one of the things I loved most about him. There were never any games to play.

"More like I need something to keep me busy."

"Careful, don't let Scott hear that."

Logan laughs. Damn it. It's still one of my favorite things to hear. "Scott already kicks my ass enough."

"Can I get you two anything to drink?" A server comes around, interrupting our conversation. He doesn't look like he could be any older than twelve. It makes me feel old.

"Hot chocolate with whipped cream and Bailey's, right?" Logan asks.

I nod.

"Make it two," Logan tells him.

It shouldn't make me as happy as it does that he remembers my drink. After my day of skiing, I need a little something extra to warm up.

This isn't something I pictured. Talking with Logan like this.

It's easy. Comfortable. Something I never expected when I got here.

"What have you been up to since you got back here?" I ask, pulling my legs up into the chair. Après-ski cozy fires are one of my favorite parts of skiing.

"Honestly? Rehab."

"Was your leg that bad?"

Logan's eyes study me. They give nothing away. It has me squirming in my seat.

"Here you go." The waiter drops off our drinks. I take mine and gulp down a too-hot sip, scalding my tongue. At least it gives me something to do other than think about the way Logan is looking at me.

A warmth spreads through me, and it's not the Bailey's doing that.

"Shit." I try to cool my tongue. This time, Logan is smiling at me when I find his gaze.

"You okay?"

"Sorry. I was colder than I thought." It's a lie and we both know it.

"Do you want the real truth or what I've been telling people?" Logan takes his own cautious sip.

"It's me, Logan. I want the truth."

Even though the way he words the question has nerves gathering in my stomach.

"It wasn't your normal break. Compound fracture. Two broken bones. We thought the one surgery was enough, but it wasn't."

This I know. When he didn't rejoin the team, there was some speculation as to why. I never dug too deep into it.

"What happened?"

"The team flew me home to Dixon. With how bad it was, I didn't want to be anywhere in Denver. It hurt too much to see everyone celebrating the win when I was in bad shape. By the time we landed, I had to be medevaced to the hospital in Jackson because I was septic."

I try to cover the gasp, but do a poor job of it. Logan's eyes are on his mug, his finger tracing the rim.

"I picked up an infection somewhere along the way and had to have emergency surgery to try and save my life.

It was pretty close there for a while, but I pulled through. And thankfully they were able to save my leg."

"Logan."

My heart catches in my throat. I never knew about this. Sure, I knew he had a lot harder of a path to recovery than I thought based on what Gemma told me, but not this.

This time, when his brown eyes meet mine, they're sad. But still hopeful.

"I had about five surgeries to repair my leg muscle. My leg was in a cage for the better part of a year."

"And your leg? It's okay now?"

Looking at Logan, you wouldn't know what he went through. Sure, his leg has scars running down it. And the skin has a faint tint to it, but nothing like what he just told me.

He nods. "It's taken about a year since my last surgery to get here, but I'm good. It's good."

"You're not just saying that to make me feel better?"

Logan lets out a sardonic laugh. "I would've given you the watered-down version if I was trying to make you feel better."

I don't think. Standing, I walk over to his chair and wrap him in an awkward hug. His shoulders tighten at my touch before relaxing.

"I'm sorry," I whisper into his ear.

Logan still smells the same. Still feels the same under my touch.

I have to bite down on my lip to keep from crying. What would've happened if Logan hadn't made it through?

It's not something I want to think about.

Because he's here. Here with me by some crazy, fucked-up circumstance that both of us are trying to heal from injuries.

"Don't feel sorry for me. I'm here. And I'm hoping that I can rejoin the team in a few weeks."

His hands find my waist, giving me a squeeze. It sends heat rippling through me.

I guess some things haven't changed.

"I wish I would've known."

"What would you have done?" Logan pulls back, crossing his arms.

"I don't know." I sit on the table in front of him. Our knees knock together.

"Sent a fruit basket?" This time, his voice is playful.

"That seems like something that says, 'Congratulations, your team just won the big game, but you're hurt. Feel better soon?'"

"See? Perfect." Just like that, the tension is gone.

"Maybe if Scott won't kill you, you can come skiing with me sometime next week."

"Really?"

"Why not?"

Because now that I'm here with him, I don't want to lose him. In the span of a few days, Logan has tilted my world on its axis. Again.

He's been the only one to be able to do that.

If this really is a second chance for both of us, I want to grab the bull by the horns.

And not waste a minute with this man.

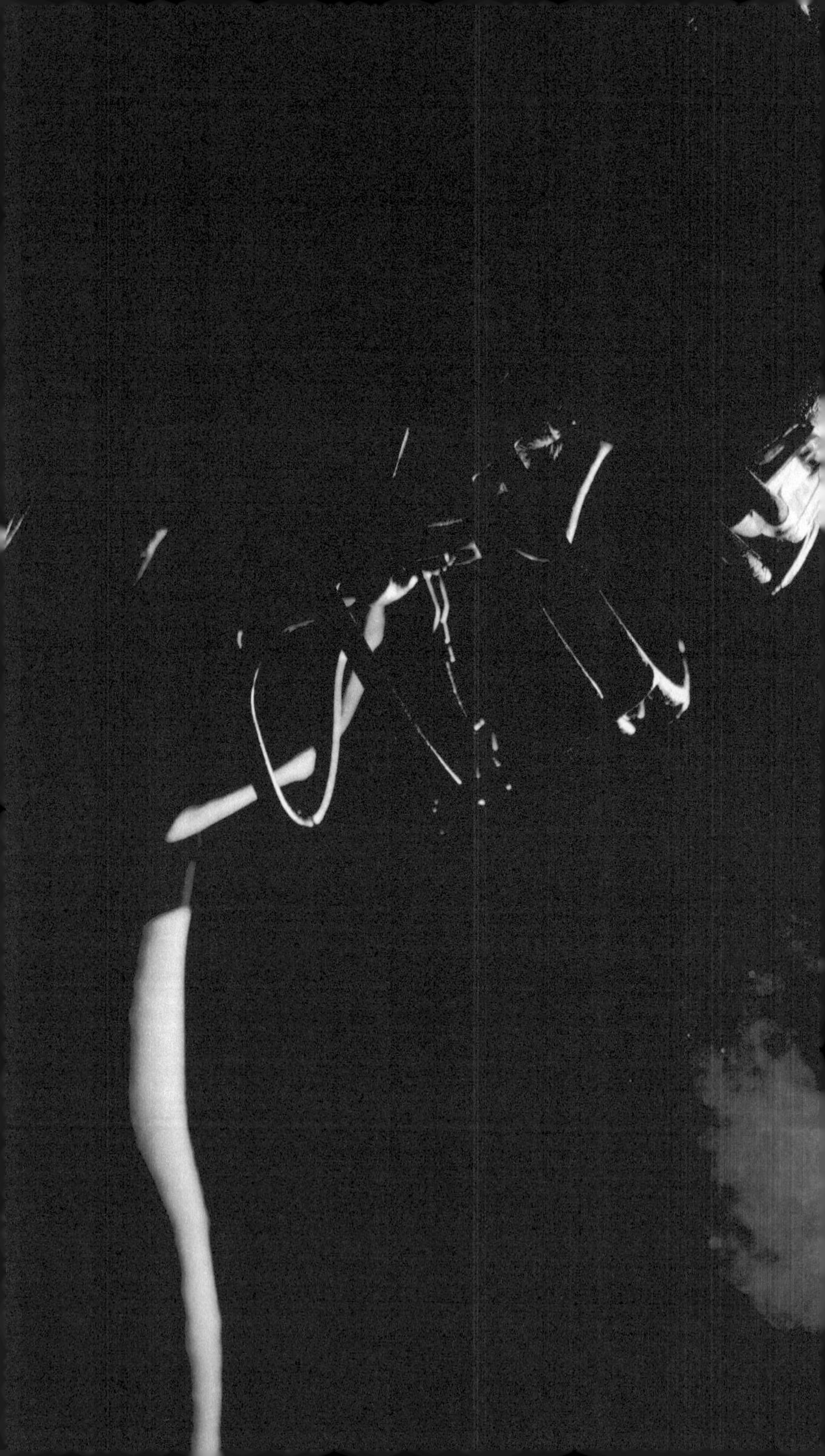

# Chapter Twelve

LOGAN

"You're awfully happy today."

Peter pins me with a look like he can't quite figure out why.

"I'm always happy."

"No, you're not." He crosses his arms, giving me what he hopes is a fierce stare. It's anything but scary.

Ever since Nash came back into his life, he's been all loved up. It's like it's starting to rub off on me too.

Things with Audrey have…softened? Ever since I told her what happened all those years ago, she doesn't look at me with contempt in her eyes.

And after the day at the ski lodge?

It's a new feeling entirely. One I hope to box up and keep ahold of a little longer.

For someone who wanted to keep me at arm's length, she's getting closer.

"Is this because of Audrey?" Peter throws the towel at my face.

"What? No." My words are more defensive than they should be.

The cocky grin that spreads across his face tells me he knows exactly what this is about. And that he will undoubtedly tell every single member of my family.

"I'm happy for you, you know. You deserve to be happy after everything. And she's always made you happy."

"Nothing's going on between the two of us."

"Between the two of whom?" Nash walks over, setting a box of new glasses down behind the bar.

"Logan and Audrey."

"No one."

We answer at the same time.

"If it's not happening yet, it totally will be." Nash shares Peter's glee.

He wasn't around yet when I brought Audrey home, but Peter has no doubt filled him in on everything that happened between the two of us.

Damn these two.

I don't want to get my hopes up, but after spending a few days with her that weren't contentious?

Fuck, my hopes are up whether I want them to be or not.

"Don't jinx it." I rap my knuckles against the bar top.

"See. You want something to happen. Admit it."

"I'm not admitting anything to you two," I grumble.

"It's okay,"—Peter ruffles my hair as I try to bat his arm away—"you don't have to tell us. We'll know."

Nash's eyes catch on something behind me and then his smile grows. "C'mon, Peter. Let's leave Logan be."

"What? Why?" He's as confused as I am.

Nash nods behind me and I spin on the stool.

Audrey.

She's bundled up, cheeks pink from the cold wind blowing through town. She looks like she just finished a run.

It shouldn't be as adorable a sight as it is, but I love seeing her like this. Here. In my town. Like she's always belonged here.

I don't know how I went so long without seeing her in person. Every time I see her, my heart feels lighter.

Seeing her immediately calms me. Like I'm drinking in fresh air for the first time in years. A reason to keep driving forward.

She's my entire reason for being.

It took all of a few weeks of being around her again to realize I can't let this chance pass me by.

Audrey was brought here for a reason. What that reason is, I don't know yet. But I know I never stopped loving her. Sure, those feelings were buried deep when we weren't together.

But never fully gone.

Peter whacks me on the shoulder, breaking me out of my thoughts.

"Audrey. Hi."

"Hi."

She tucks a piece of dark hair behind her ear. I still can't get over seeing her like this. Somehow, her with dark hair is even sexier.

"What are you doing here?"

"Really, bro?" Peter pipes up from behind the bar. I give him a cutting glare, but he smiles back at me before shifting his focus to the woman that has all of mine. "Hi, Audrey."

"Hi, Peter. It's good to see you."

"You too. How's training going for you?"

Audrey steps up to the bar, resting her crossed arms on the gleaming wood top.

"It's good. Hit some new slopes here in Dixon and it felt good. Hoping to get back to racing soon."

"Think you'll be ready for the games next year?"

"I hope so." She nods. "I called in a pickup order."

"Great. I'll go check on it for you. Good seeing you."

"You too." Audrey's eyes slide onto me as she drops down next to me. "I figured you'd be at Scott's today."

"Have the day off."

"I'm heading there soon."

"Your leg feeling good?"

"After getting out on the slopes, yeah." Her eyes are bright, practically sparkling with diamonds. "Felt really good."

"All part of the process."

She rests her head on her fist, eyeing me. "I'm guessing you had your fair share of setbacks?"

"Every time it felt like I was making some progress, it seemed like I took a giant leap backward. It fucking sucked."

"You're looking good now."

"You noticed?" I quirk a brow at her.

Ever since she showed up at Scott's gym, I've been pushing myself a little harder. Getting an extra set in. Adding a little more weight.

I want to impress the woman whose heart I broke all those years ago. Show her that I'm still the same guy.

"Everyone in there notices you."

"I don't care about everyone."

Her eyes widen a fraction. I could get lost in those deep brown orbs of hers. The way she bites down on her bottom lip. I notice everything about her.

*Everything.*

She's the only person I have eyes for.

"Logan, I—"

"Here you go," Peter interrupts.

Damn it. If only he took a bit longer getting her order.

"I'll see you tomorrow." Audrey smiles at me before grabbing her earbuds to pop in her ears.

"You will."

God, everything about this is turning me back into the bumbling idiot I was when I first met her.

"Could you have picked a worse time to come back?" I hiss. Sometimes my brother is so lost in his own world that he doesn't catch on to things.

"You said it wasn't about her," he argues. "Which, it totally is, by the way."

"Stop it."

"Hey Audrey!" Peter calls out.

"What are you doing?"

Fucking interfering family.

"Yeah?" She pulls an earbud out of her ear.

"You two want to test out one of the new igloos we got for the roof later this week?" Peter asks. "It'd really be helping us out."

It takes everything I have not to groan at my interfering brother. I feel like I'm back in high school and can't get a girl to go out with me on my own.

Audrey's eyes flick between the two of us.

"Me and Logan?"

"Yeah." His grin is huge.

Audrey looks to me with a small smile on her face. "Sure."

Yes? She said yes?

Shit, if I'd known it'd be that easy, I might have done it sooner.

Or, you know, not have my brother do it for me.

Peter elbows me, knocking me out of my shock.

"Great. I'll text you."

Audrey doesn't say anything, giving me another one of those smiles before leaving that hits me in the gut.

"You should be thanking me." Peter points at me.

"Why?"

"Because she clearly wanted you to ask her out and you didn't."

I roll my eyes at him. "We have a history. I have to take it slow."

"If I took things slow with Nash, he might not be here right now. You needed a push."

"Didn't we already test the igloos?" I give him a skeptical look.

"Of course we did,"—he rolls his eyes at me—"but I need to know if they're romantic. I can cancel if you want."

"Please don't!" I shout.

"Knew it. You're so far gone for her."

"Yeah, yeah."

Except he's not wrong. Maybe my brother giving me the push is exactly what I needed.

I guess there are worse things than interfering family.

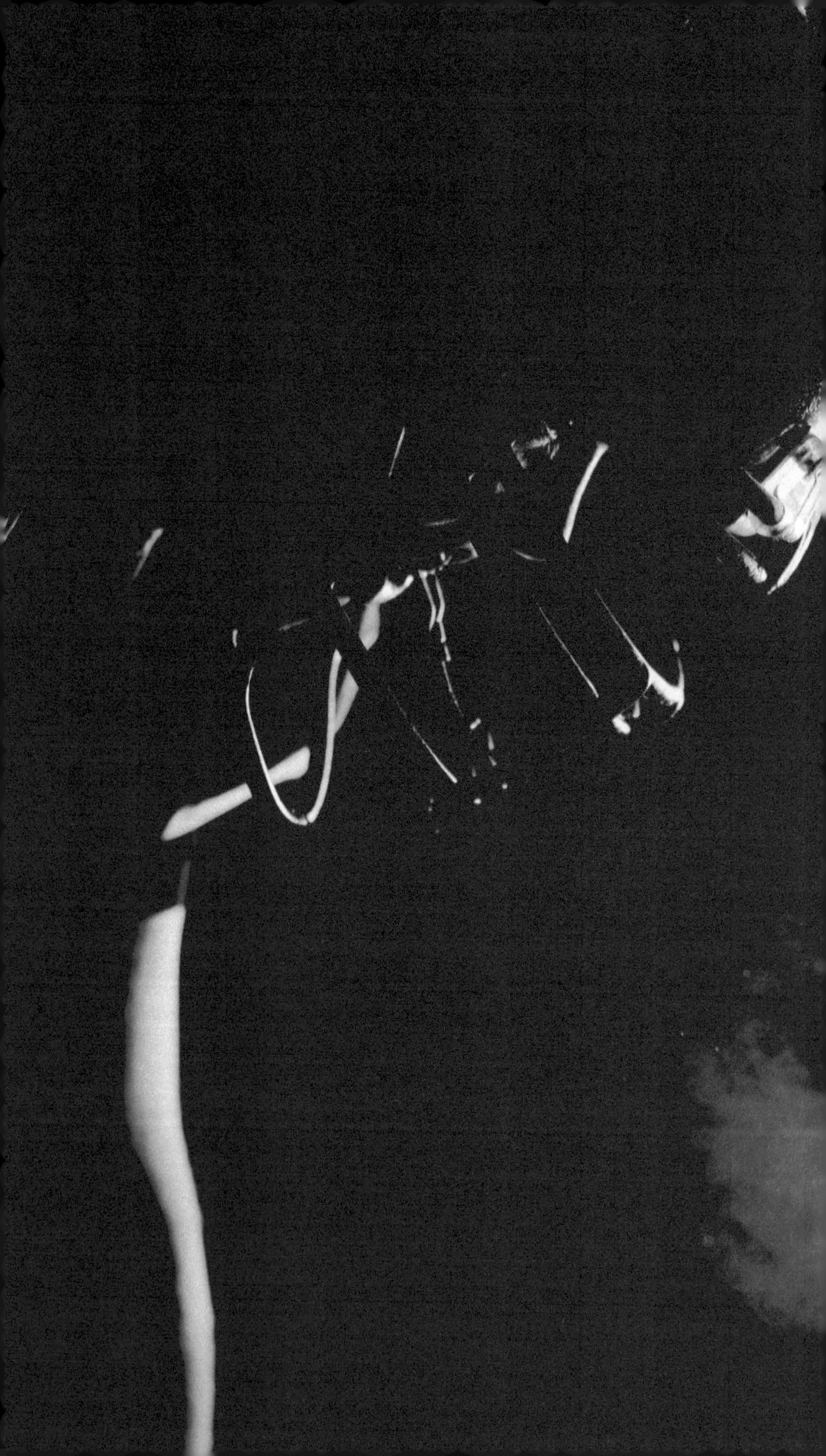

# Chapter Thirteen

## LOGAN

"Is everything ready?" I ask Nash.

He chucks the towel in his hand at me. "You've asked me thirteen times now it seems. Yes, it's ready."

I blow out a nervous breath. "This is my first date with Audrey. Everything has to be perfect."

"First date?" Nash quirks a brow at me.

The bar is quiet for a Thursday night. It helps calm my nerves. Because if everything blows up in my face, then no one will see me leaving on my own tonight.

If all does go to plan, I hope Audrey will let me have a second date. And a third.

"Shut up." I toss the towel back at him. "You know what I mean."

"I do. And I know exactly how you feel."

"Shit, you do."

Nash left without a word nine years ago. With his sudden reappearance, he threw my brother for a loop. Now, the two of them are stronger than ever.

Something I hope will be the case for Audrey and me.

Damn. Did it just get hot in here?

"It's going to be weird. As long as you acknowledge it, you'll be fine. And at least you won't have the whole town staring at you."

"I guess we have that going for us."

"Be thankful." Nash points a finger at me. "What drinks do you want and I'll get them started?"

"Two hot chocolates with Bailey's, please."

It's Audrey's favorite. And perfect for tonight.

"Wow. Drinking something other than the Clara? I didn't know you could."

"Don't judge what I'm drinking. Maybe I'll mix it up with the IPA later."

"Sure."

Nash grabs the ingredients and starts expertly mixing the cocktails when a hand comes down on my shoulder.

"Logan Winchester. As I live and breathe."

"Coach Snider." I wrap my arms around my old football coach. "It's good to see you."

"You've been back in town for almost two years and never stopped by to say hi?"

I scrub a hand over the back of my neck, nerves settling in.

Coach Snider was one of my biggest supporters. He was there for me at my first college game and again for my first game with the Mountain Lions.

When I got back to town, he was the last person I wanted to see. I felt like a failure. Like what happened to me was somehow my fault.

"Little preoccupied." I pat my leg for good measure.

"I'm not buying that, but I'll let it slide." He pins me with a stare. His dark brown eyes hold a laugh that I'm thankful for. Even at his age, he still looks as young as ever. "How's rehab going?"

"I'm hoping I'll be ready to start playing in a few weeks."

"Really?" He looks shocked.

When I tell most people that, they're gung ho with excitement. Everyone loves a comeback story, right? I'm hoping mine will be the best one this town has ever seen.

"Scott says I'm on track. We'll see." I rap my knuckles on the wooden bar in front of me for good measure.

"Cut that superstitious shit. If you're putting in the work, then it'll show. And here I was thinking I might get you to stick around."

"Stick around?" I lean back in my seat, staring at my old coach.

"I'll be retiring at the end of this year."

"What?" Surprise laces my voice. "You're an institution. You've been at Dixon High since…well, forever."

He claps me on the shoulder, waving down one of the bartenders for his own drink. "Wife is ready for it. Kids are grown with babies and we want to travel. There is more to life than football."

"Really?" I laugh.

"You might not think it, but there truly is. I was hoping I could convince you to take my job."

"Me? Coach?"

There's no way.

Coach Snider and Coach Brooks are two of the best coaches out there. There's no way I can ever match up to the two of them.

Me? A coach?

It's laughable.

"You're good. You have a keen eye for plays and openings when others don't. I was hoping you'd want to teach the next generation."

"Really?"

"If you're playing, I guess not." He grabs his drink. "It was good seeing you, Logan. Don't be a stranger."

"Thanks, Coach." I give him a quick slap on the back before he rejoins his group.

His earlier words have completely jumbled my brain.

Even before my injury, I never considered coaching. Coach Brooks was one of the most cerebral men I've ever met. Always watching, never putting himself in the center of the room. I don't see myself like that.

"You okay?" Nash asks, setting two steaming mugs in front of me.

"Yeah."

He sets a shot glass on the wooden bar and pours tequila in it. "You look like you could use this.

Shit. I grab the tiny glass and down it.

Now my nerves are even more frayed, and Audrey isn't even here yet.

"Send her up when she gets here?" Grabbing the drinks in hand, I head up the stairs.

The cool night air hits me the second I walk out the door.

Thank fuck. It helps calm my raging nerves.

Between the coach's words and waiting on Audrey, I'm buzzing.

And not off the alcohol.

The roof looks even better than it did the last time. With all of the twinkle lights on, it's the perfect setting for a first date.

Or a second first date, in this case.

With the years that have gone by, I'm hoping we can start fresh. Something new.

Like Nash said, it'll be awkward. Even though Audrey said yes, I could see the pain still there. Pain I put there. Even if I was doing it for the right reasons.

Since the roof still isn't open to the public, there's only one igloo operating tonight. Peter and Nash really pulled out all the stops. A bouquet of flowers sits on the table with a tray full of s'mores fixings.

I hope to be snuggled up with Audrey in front of the fire soon.

This couldn't be more perfect.

"Hey Logan."

Here goes nothing.

# Chapter Fourteen



"Are you sure this looks okay?" I ask Lily. Again.

"You look gorgeous, babe. Logan won't know what hit him."

I smooth my hand over the black sweater dress I'm wearing. With the knee-high heeled brown boots, it should be warm enough tonight. But the way these boots hug my legs? I'm hoping it'll drive Logan wild.

Because no matter what I keep telling myself, tonight is a big deal.

It's more than just a night out.

It's a first date with Logan.

The only man I've ever truly loved. It would be nerve-racking for anyone.

Butterflies have been ever present in my stomach since Logan asked me out. Well, Peter. It felt like I was back in high school again being asked on a date for the first time.

Except there's more pressure.

I want everything to be perfect. Right down to my

outfit. Not that Logan would care if I show up in a potato sack.

"Okay, thanks, Lily."

"And don't forget the condoms!" she sings before ending the video call.

"Lily!"

Damn it.

The last thing I need is to be thinking about sex with Logan.

Sex was never the issue. Just thinking about it has me clenching my legs. He always had a healthy sex drive. What guy isn't?

My pleasure was always his first concern. I'd never had that with any guy I'd been with. It was never boring. Logan loved coming up with new games to keep it spicy.

Something I never once minded.

Pushing thoughts of our sex life to the side, I spritz on perfume and give myself one final look in the mirror.

It's still strange seeing my naturally blonde hair dyed almost black.

Never in a million years did I think I would be here, rehabbing my knee in a tiny town in Wyoming and seeing Logan again.

I crank up the music in the car, letting myself get lost in the music as I slowly drive the well-traveled road, familiar since I've been here so many times with Logan.

I need the time to settle my nerves before I get to Dixon.

My brain still hasn't quite wrapped itself around being near him. I knew this was where he grew up. Hell, I visited here with him and met his family. I guess my brain was in survival mode when I was sent here.

Turning down the best people in the business would've

been a mistake. A big one. With the games coming so soon, I have to make smart choices.

I only hope giving Logan Winchester a second chance is a *smart choice.*

The drive feels like it goes by quickly, and before I know it, I'm pulling into the parking lot behind the bar.

The Tipsy Cocktail is quiet as I open the door. It's everything a bar in a small town should be. High ceilings. Lots of natural night. A bar that wraps around the entire place with patrons scattered among the tables.

"Hi. Welcome to The Tipsy Cocktail. Just one tonight?" a girl with a bright white smile and red hair asks me.

"I'm actually meeting someone here."

"Audrey!"

Spinning toward the sound of my name, an easy smile erupts onto my face. "Peter."

Peter was always my favorite brother of Logan's. The quieter of the Winchester family, he easily accepted me into the fold the first time I visited. Not that his other family members didn't, but Peter was the first one I met and I loved his subdued nature.

"It's so good to see you." He wraps me in a warm hug. "I didn't get to say a proper hello the other day."

"You were busy."

"Giving Logan a hard time," he laughs.

"Nothing new at all then."

Peter's laugh quiets. "He is really excited to see you again."

"Me too." I'd be lying if I said otherwise. "Is he here?"

"He's on the roof. Follow me." Peter shows me to a side door at the end of the bar. "Upstairs. If you need anything, we'll be up to check on you soon."

"Will do. Thank you."

"Don't be a stranger." He winks and leaves me.

Taking a deep breath, I head up the stairs, not knowing what awaits me. What I'm greeted with is far more incredible than I ever could have imagined.

String lights hang from poles that line the edge of the roof. Four igloos adorn the roof. There's enough space between them to give each group privacy.

But tonight? Tonight it's me and the man walking toward me.

"Hey Logan."

"I'm glad you could make it." Logan's voice betrays him. He sounds as nervous as I feel. "Pretty nice setup, right?"

*Glad I'm not the only one.*

"It's no Screaming Moose, but I guess it'll do."

"Thanks for humoring me then."

There's a happy expression on his face that I've missed. The smile he wears makes him even more handsome. And that's saying something since those jeans hug his thighs and the gray quarter-zip sweater molds to him.

"This is amazing. Peter really outdid himself."

Logan holds out his hand and I link hands with him. The contact sends sparks racing up my arm. The chemistry with Logan was never a problem.

"This is our hut tonight."

Logan holds the door open and lets me in first. Two Adirondack chairs sit facing a small fire, blankets hanging off the back. A small tray of food sits on the table between the chairs, as well as two steaming mugs.

With the sun long since set, it couldn't be more romantic.

"Wow."

I drop into one of the chairs, sitting close to the edge to get all the heat from the fire.

"Hot chocolate?" Logan hands me one of the mugs. "Added a shot of Bailey's to keep us warm."

"Thank you." I hold my mug up to him. "What are we toasting to?"

Logan clinks his mug against mine, but doesn't move it. "To fresh starts."

"To fresh starts."

It's music to my ears as I take a large gulp. Not too hot. It's perfect.

"I'm nervous as fuck." Setting his drink down, he rubs his hands down his jeans.

"Does it help that I am too?"

His gaze rolls over me, from the top of my head to the tips of my boots. "You don't look nervous. You look fucking gorgeous as ever."

"Trust me, I was. Still am." I take another warm sip. "This was the third outfit change."

"Maybe we should've toasted to our nerves."

"Fresh starts mean no nerves," I tell him.

"Am I allowed to tell you how nervous I was on our first date? I mean, before?"

I suck in a breath, waiting for the pain to hit when I think of us in the past. But it doesn't come. Maybe this really is our fresh start.

"Nervous about little ol' me?" I say with a Southern accent.

"Fuck yeah. You are the most badass person I'd ever met. Still are, for that matter."

"Not quite there yet."

Logan leans back in his chair, giving me an assessing stare. He looks relaxed, at ease now. "Who would've thought we'd both be here at this point in our lives?"

My laugh is sardonic. "Certainly not me."

"More than just one kind of fresh start, I guess."

He's right. And the more I'm around him, the easier it is to slip into our new roles. I don't carry the same anger toward him that I once did.

Logan never hated me, he just left me.

But that's in the past.

"Can I interest you in a s'more?"

"Can you?" I laugh. "Of course."

Logan readies a stick for me and hands it over. When I grab it from him, he doesn't let go. The contact from him does more to warm me than the small fire in front of us.

"This is really nice." Logan huddles closer to the fire.

Quiet settles over us as we each toast our marshmallows. Eat our s'mores. Hide our smiles when we're caught looking at each other.

The darker it gets, the more I'm pulled under the spell of this evening.

The igloo.

The s'mores.

The fire.

Logan.

It's about as perfect as you can get for a fresh start.

A shiver racks my body, the cold finally becoming too much for me. Logan notices immediately.

Standing, he reaches behind me and drapes the blanket over my shoulders. He doesn't let go. It's as if he's trying to hold me to him. Keep in all our warmth so we don't lose this moment between us.

It has my stomach swooping.

This is what I remember most about being with Logan. The way he always made me feel. We were together for so long that the feeling should have gone away. But it didn't. Everything always felt new with him.

Logan drops his forehead to mine. I'm not breathing.

Butterflies are erupting in my stomach. All I want is for Logan to lean forward and close the distance.

To remember what it feels like to have his lips on mine. To get caught up in kissing when we have all the time in the world.

I bet he would taste sweet, like the s'mores we've been eating and the hot chocolate we've been drinking.

He's right there, inches from me. I could make the first move. Kiss him.

I move in, ever so slowly, before the door to the igloo bangs open.

"More hot chocolate."

Logan leaps back, knocking the half-empty s'mores tray off the table at Nash's sudden appearance.

"Shit." He looks embarrassed.

"Sorry, did I interrupt?" Nash's eyes dart between the two of us. "I thought you might be ready for more drinks. It's been a while."

Logan scrubs his hand down the back of his neck. He's nervous now that Nash is here.

"I'm just going to drop these off and let you two get back to it. Logan, text if you need anything." Nash sets the fresh drinks down and hurries out.

"Well, that was embarrassing." Logan stoops to clean up the remainder of the marshmallows and graham crackers.

"It's okay." I let out a deep, nervous chuckle.

"God. It wasn't even this bad when I was living with them."

Dropping down next to him, I help him clean up. "Brought a lot of girls home when you stayed with them?"

Logan grabs my hands.

"No one. There was no one." The fierce look in his

eyes tell me it's imperative I believe him. But the one thing Logan never has been is a liar.

Well, except that one time.

But I'm not going to focus on that.

"I can imagine the two of them catching you. God, the grief they'd give you."

Logan laughs now, knowing I'm not mad. "They'd tell every single member of my family."

"Mason would be the worst."

"Why do older brothers always have that way about them?"

And just like that, the night goes back to how it was before that kiss. Almost kiss.

As much as I want it to happen, it's for the best it didn't. I'll be leaving soon.

It's fine.

Totally fine.

Except damn it, I really wanted him to kiss me.

# Chapter Fifteen

## AUDREY

"You two just need to bang already."

"Lily!"

My head whips around, like everyone in the Jackson area heard her comment. It's still early, and with snow blanketing the town this morning, everyone is heading to the slopes.

I wish that were me. Maybe this afternoon if I'm lucky.

But I have a session with Scott today. And if I am *really* lucky? Logan.

"Don't *Lily* me. It's Logan we're talking about. You had a date. You almost kissed!"

If only Nash hadn't interrupted us. I wanted nothing more than to feel his lips on mine. Out of all the things I missed about him, his kisses were definitely high on the list.

We'd spend hours making out. We could never get enough of each other. The way his lips would touch mine ignited every cell in my body. Logan was an expert kisser.

Nipping.

Sucking.

Teasing.

Just the thought of it now has me wanting to find him and put myself out of my misery.

"I don't want to rush this."

"Any slower and you'll be going backward."

The gym is in sight ahead. I'm glad I'm staying so close. These morning walks are usually a time to clear my head. Today though, I needed sound advice from a friend.

Or whatever Lily is telling me to do now.

"I'm only here a few more weeks, Lily. There's no point in starting anything."

"That was your excuse in Switzerland too."

"Hey. I was heartbroken then."

"And when you were ready to start dating?" If this were a video call, I can picture exactly the look she'd be giving me. Calling me on my bullshit.

"Okay, fine. But I really will only be here for a few more weeks."

"Casual sex then."

"Nothing with Logan has ever been casual. I'm not about to start now."

"You're killing me, Audrey. Just imagine how good it would be. You always said it was the best sex of your life."

"I regret telling you that."

"No you don't. Now, be a dear and bag Logan so I can live vicariously through you."

She hangs up before I can get another word in.

Some best friend she is.

Except…she's not wrong.

All I've been thinking about since our date is that almost kiss. About wanting more with Logan. Being with him now and remembering the memories from before is creating a storm of emotions in me.

Do I want more with him? Yes.

Wrapped up with him in that igloo felt like we could

start something new. That we could move on from the past and start over.

I want that. More than I ever thought possible.

But I'm still wary. A crushed heart will do that to you.

Pushing into the gym, I'm met with a wall of heat and noise, warming me down to my bones.

And the man who is absorbing my every thought is laid out on the mat, stretching. Watching the delicious way his thighs strain against his shorts does nothing to quell the thoughts stirring inside me.

"Hey Audrey."

Heather's voice startles me.

"Hi."

"Looking at anything interesting?"

"No," I answer too quickly.

"Right." She gives me the side-eye, clearly not believing me. "Scott's got some exercises for you today. Short day, then you can hit the slopes."

"Fine by me."

Any day spent skiing is a good day in my books.

I only need to make it through the morning here, not ogling Logan, to get there. Which is easier said than done after I hang up my coat and make my way over to Scott.

"Audrey. Glad you're here. I've got something different for you two today."

"Great."

It's not like I can argue with him. He knows this stuff the best.

Logan's waiting on the other side of him. His eyes take a slow perusal of me from head to toe. I feel it everywhere.

How can one glance from this man make me want to throw all common sense out the window and do the one thing my body craves?

"I want you both on the block. You'll each hold on to

the ball, and the first to drop loses. Sounds easy enough, but it'll help build your balance. We'll do a few rounds and then hit the treadmills. Sound good?"

"Works for me." Logan steps up to the small box that we'll be standing on. I mirror his stance. "Want to make a bet out of this?"

Propping my hands on my hips, I stare him down. "What do you have in mind?"

"Can you two do anything without making a bet on it?"

"No." We answer Scott at the same time.

"Fine. Get in position." Scott holds the medicine ball out between the two of us as we step onto the wooden platform.

"Ready?"

Each of us grabs onto the ball. The slightest brush of his fingertips against mine has goose bumps breaking out on my skin.

I really hate that he still has this effect on me.

So much for trying to play it cool.

"Go."

Scott drops his hold on the ball and my grip tightens. I used to hate these kinds of exercises. But now I love them. Using this body, feeling myself regain lost strength—it's a powerful feeling.

"About this bet…" Logan stares down at me.

I'm on high alert being this close to him. The soft smell of his soap. His gentle touch. The way his eyes are fixed on mine and unmoving.

If I weren't as far along in my recovery, it'd throw me. Have me faltering immediately.

But I don't.

My competitive streak is alive and well. And I want to use it to best Logan Winchester.

"What do you care to wager?"

"How about another date?" He quirks a brow down at me.

"That's too easy."

"So you want another date then?" His mouth pulls up in a smile.

Damn it. I played my hand too easily.

"I want something else."

The tip of Logan's finger brushes over mine. It sends a thrill racing through me.

"Stop trying to throw me off my game."

"I'm doing no such thing."

He dips his head closer. His warm breath ghosts over my cheek. "Then tell me what you want if I lose."

What do I want?

I want another date with him. I want to spend time with him. I want... God, I want everything he'll give me right now.

I want...

A lightbulb goes off.

One that will hopefully mean I win this game and bring Logan to his knees.

"Remember those games we used to play?" I quirk a brow at him.

He growls, his hold slipping ever so slightly.

*Oh yeah, he remembers.*

"That's what I want."

"If I lose," Logan starts, "you want to play one of our old games?"

My gaze never strays from his. I can see his eyes widen at what my words mean.

There's no denying this thing between us. Over the last few weeks, Logan has torn down every wall I put up, reminding me of one simple fact.

I want him. It's always been him. And I want to spend every second I can with him until I head back to Colorado.

"Scared?"

Logan laughs, shifting his balance ever so slightly.

"No. I don't think you know what a bet is. It sounds like we're both winning here."

"Maybe I'm just trying to get you to lose."

"You should know by now, Audrey,"—Logan leans in, his lips by my ears sending shockwaves racing through me —"I'll do anything to win."

"And what do you get if you win?" This time, it's my voice that's breathy.

When he speaks again, his lips brush my ear. It's almost enough to send me falling to the mat, but I right myself just in time. "Remember that night in Lake Placid?"

Do I ever… It was the single hottest night of my life. I had a competition and Logan had a bye week. It was one of the few times he was able to come meet me during the season.

My legs falter under the memory. The way Logan worshipped my body. Sent me spiraling to heights I never dreamed of hitting.

"I want that."

Logan pulls back and I shift toward him, like if I don't stay connected to him, I'll lose him again.

It's the smallest of movements. But it's enough of a move that has both of us losing our balance. Except Logan tries to overcorrect and falls off the step right on his ass.

"Yes! I win!" I hold the ball up before jumping down to get in Logan's face. "Looks like you lost."

Holding out a hand, I help Logan up off the mat. He doesn't let go.

"Are either one of us really losing here, Audrey?"

My thighs clench together at the way his voice comes out.

Being here like this with Logan was the furthest thing from my mind when I landed in Jackson. All I wanted was some space to train and get back to racing shape before the games.

Now, with Logan here, my mind—and my heart—are being pulled in two different directions. Can I have it all again?

"Hey Audrey. Got a call for you." Scott comes over, handing me the gym's phone. I recognize the number on the screen.

"Hang on." I throw up a finger toward Logan and head to find a spot with more privacy.

"Hey, Coach."

"Audrey. How you feeling?"

No beating around the bush. He gets straight to the point.

"Good. Leg feels strong."

"Glad to hear it. Because you've got a race next weekend."

"What?" My gaze flits to Logan's. He's watching me as I pull back into the corner by the lockers. Like I don't want him to hear this conversation.

I'm not ready to leave him.

"We didn't think you'd be ready, but I called to talk with Scott and he says you're doing great." Of course the two of them are talking and he's keeping Coach updated on my status. "Seeing as how the race is here, we figured it'd be a great chance for you to get back out there."

"I thought the qualifiers weren't until January?" I'm trying to think of any excuse not to leave this weekend.

"Why wait if you're ready? With you being out most of

the year, you need some events under your belt—so to speak—to get there."

Shit.

I didn't really think about that. I'd been so focused on getting back into shape, that I never stopped to think about what I would need to do to even get there.

Shit.

"When do I need to be back in town?"

"Need you here next Thursday."

It's Wednesday. More than a full week to get home. Not an impossible ask. Except my mind is already flying ahead to this weekend and cashing in on my bet with Logan.

My heart catches in my chest.

This is what happened last time. With our crazy schedules and me constantly being sent all over the world to train and race, we were like two ships passing in the night. And with Logan looking to rejoin the team, what will that mean for us?

I only just got him back. The thought of losing him again has my hand rubbing over the spot in my chest where my heart lies.

I don't want to lose him again.

I *can't* lose him again.

So much for taking this slow.

"Audrey? You still with me?"

"Yeah. Sounds good. I'll see you Thursday."

I hang up the phone without a second thought, squeezing it in my palms.

"What was that all about?" Logan's voice startles me.

"I've got a race next weekend," I tell him. My tone is cautious. I don't want to spook him. This thing between us, while familiar, is still new. I don't want to do anything that might cause him to get cold feet.

"Audrey, that's great."

"Yeah." I tuck a loose strand of hair behind my ear. "It's at Copper Mountain."

"Oh." His face drops, that momentary happiness for me wiped away. "When will you be leaving Jackson?"

"Need to be there Thursday, so might give myself a few days to adjust being back home."

"Right, sounds like a good plan."

"You two ready to go again?" Scott interrupts us.

"Ready as I'll ever be." I slap the phone down in his outstretched hand and follow Logan back to where we were.

This time, there's no playful teasing. We're quiet, neither one of us quite knowing what to say or do.

It seems like just yesterday I landed in Jackson. That I reconnected with Logan. I fought him those first weeks, not wanting anything to do with him.

Now? Now I don't want to go.

My heart is in Dixon.

With Logan.

Where I always left it.

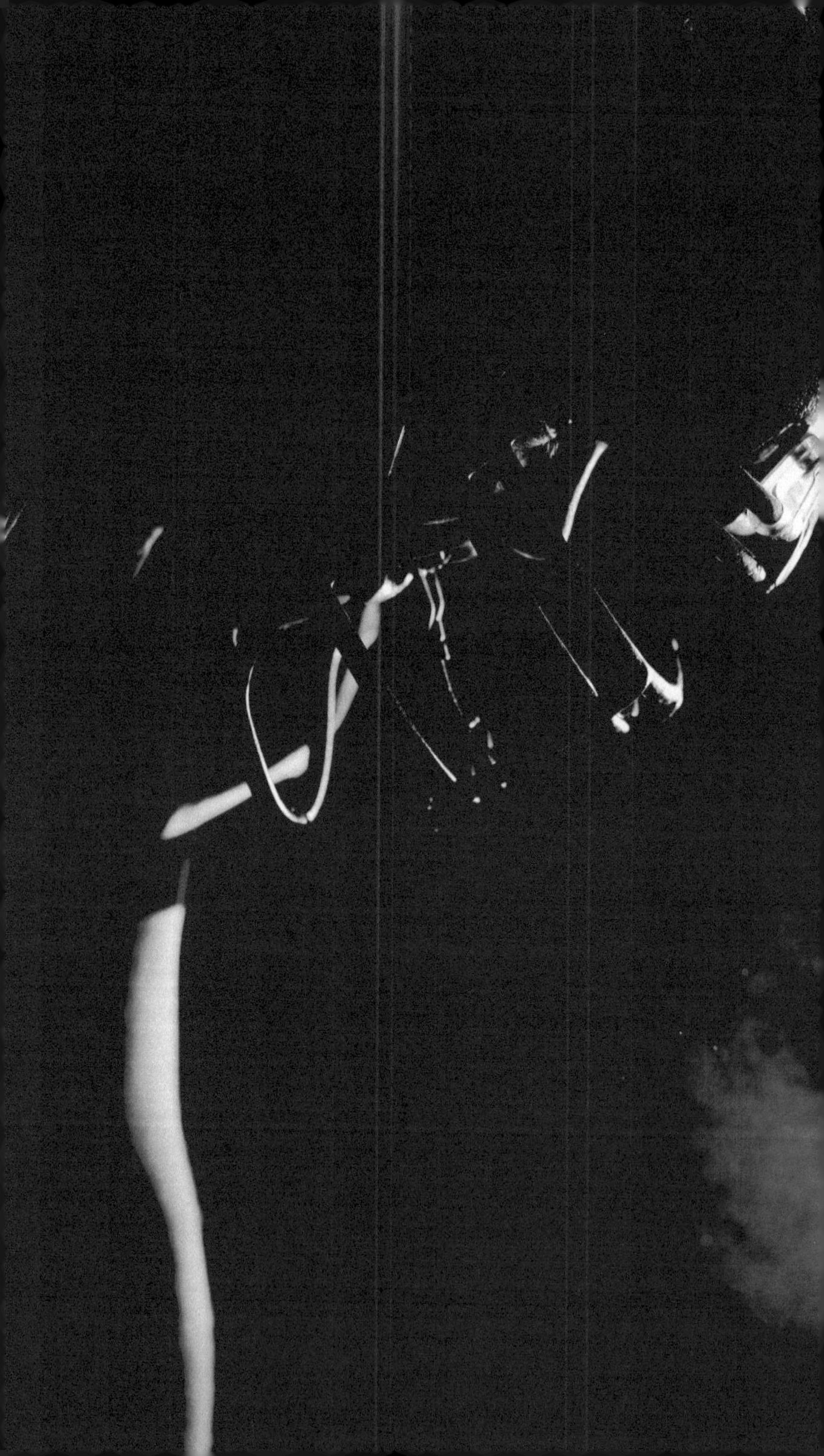

# Chapter Sixteen



"Did you burn the popcorn?"

"You forgot it was in there!"

"Me? You were supposed to be watching it."

The sounds of my brothers arguing greet me as I elbow my way into Mason's house, loaded down with tonight's dinner.

Stacks of shoes line the small entryway. Ever since Ivy moved in with him, he's outnumbered. It's like the two women in his life have multiplied everything.

It's comforting, in a way. Seeing my big brother find this kind of happiness gives me hope that I can have the same.

Hopefully with Audrey.

Just the thought of her name sends me reeling.

She's leaving. Going back to Copper Mountain.

I knew this was temporary. She was only supposed to be here for a short while.

Train. Rehab. Home to Colorado.

Just like me. Except with fewer setbacks.

When Nash spots me, he looks relieved.

"Thank God you brought food. These two are useless."

I set the pizza boxes on the counter.

"It's your fault," Mason grumbles, opening the box and grabbing a slice.

"How do you two manage?" I laugh, shaking my head.

"Peter."

"Ivy."

They answer over each other.

"It's popcorn. I'm sure even you two can manage to figure it out."

"If I'd known I'd be attacked like this in my own house, I would've thought twice before inviting you guys over."

"Please." Peter brings the drinks inside. Snow sticks to his coat. Winter weather has hit full force, the cold clinging to every part of me as it settles in Dixon. "You would've just moped because Ivy and Willow are gone."

"Not true."

There's no force behind his words. With Willow heading to her mom's soon—now that she's home from her overseas tour—I know he's already missing her.

"I'd say I'd invite you to my place," I tell them, "but Layla's old apartment is smaller than a shoebox."

I was able to lease her small studio over her old store. Now that she's living in London, it was sitting empty. And it was about time I moved out of my brother's and let him get on with his life.

He and Nash deserve some time together after I spent so many months with them.

"Willow would say it's the perfect spot for a fort."

"Well, if you and Ivy need a night alone, I'll take her."

I love my niece. She's the fucking best.

"Nah. I'm already going through withdrawal, and they're only gone for a few hours tonight."

Ivy took Willow out for a girls' night with my sister.

Both of them are trying to spend as much time as they can with her. I know Mason doesn't mind that Willow gets this time with her mom, but after being her only parent here for so long, it makes it that much harder.

"Any sign of Blake yet?" Peter asks, grabbing plates and carrying the pizza into the living room.

"He texted he'd be late. We can start eating without him." I drop down onto the small sofa that takes up most of the space in his living room. For a growing family, Mason doesn't have a lot of sitting room.

It's times like this I wish I had this kind of life with Audrey.

No expectations. No races or games.

A quiet life in Dixon. Only the two of us.

God, she's only been here a few weeks, and I'm picturing a life with her. I'm not ready for her to go.

"What's with the face?" Mason nudges me.

"I'm not making a face."

"You totally are," Nash confirms.

If I can't talk to my brothers, who can I talk to about this?

"Audrey's leaving."

"What?" Three sets of eyes stare back at me.

"Already?"

"When?"

"But why?"

They fire questions at me, left and right. I try to take it all in, but it's hard to focus. Because the only thing consuming me is Audrey.

"Why's she leaving again?" Mason asks.

"Is it really leaving if she's going home?" Peter asks, kicking his feet up on Mason's coffee table.

Mason shoves his feet off, grabbing a bottle of beer and taking a large gulp.

"The fact still remains. Audrey is leaving," I point out.

"Leaving Logan…again."

"Leaving Jackson," I correct.

"Tomato, *to-mah-to*," Nash tells me. "She's still leaving you."

The crack widens in my chest. I thought this was our chance, but I had hoped we would have more time before she left. A new beginning for the two of us. Turns out, we're heading straight down the same road we took before.

Are we going to crash and burn again?

"And what do you suggest I do?"

"What did I miss?" Blake bursts in the door, stomping off his boots. "Sorry, there was an issue on set, and now the snow is really coming down."

"Logan is in love with Audrey," Peter tells him.

"I thought we already knew that." He drops into the beanbag that sits in front of the TV. "You know, if you're going to have us over, you really should invest in better furniture," Blake complains as he wiggles around, trying to get comfortable.

"You didn't have to come."

"And miss this?" He cracks open a Clara that he brought with him. "Never. I love the Winchester family craziness."

"Hey!" we all shout at the same time.

"What? I include myself in this now too."

This is one of the things I love about my siblings partnering off. I love that our family is growing. I love Blake. He's the perfect guy for Gemma. And Simon is perfect for Layla. Even if he took her to London.

"Can you go with her?" Peter states it like it's the obvious solution.

"It wouldn't work."

"Why not?" Blake asks, taking a bite of pizza. "What's keeping you here?"

"Well…"

What is keeping me here? At this point, my leg is as good as it's going to get. It's a matter of ripping off the Band-Aid and meeting with the team.

It's the last step in my road to recovery. To regain my place with the Mountain Lions. It's so close, I can taste it.

But I'm nervous.

What if things don't go my way?

"What about you guys?"

Mason waves me off. "We're not going anywhere, Logan."

"What if she doesn't want me to go with her?"

"You'll never know if you don't ask," Blake tells me. "Trust me, if you love her, you don't want to let her get away."

"It's only a few weeks, right?" Nash asks.

"At this point, I guess."

Of course, if she qualifies, then it'd be more races. Press. Events.

"Jesus, Logan. Grow a pair and just go with her. It's not like you're committing to marriage," Peter huffs out.

"Good to know where you stand on marriage," Nash tells him.

"Not with you," he tries to correct.

"When are you two going to get married?" Blake waves a finger between the two of them.

Now both of them look stunned.

The night carries on like usual with us. A hockey game —the Colorado Black Diamonds—is on in the background. No one is paying attention as we're all arguing or talking about something.

None of us notice how late it is until Ivy comes in the house, a sleeping Willow in her arms.

"I thought you weren't going to be home for another hour." Mason jumps up, pulling her into a hug.

"The snow is picking up, so we left early. Besides, Willow fell asleep during the movie. Too much ice cream."

"Need me to put her down?"

She shakes her head. "I've got her. Have fun with your brothers."

They share a look. And when Mason turns back to us, his expression tells us it's time to get going.

"Alright. I love you guys, but time to go."

"I guess that means my wife should be at home too."

"Gross, Blake," Peter tells him.

"What?" He throws his hands up in defense. "I haven't seen her all day."

"Seriously. That's our sister."

"I didn't say anything. I don't know how I put up with you guys."

Peter and Nash give Blake grief as they head out to their cars.

"You okay?" Mason stops me before I can leave.

"I don't know."

"Even if she leaves, you'll be okay. You survived. You've been through hell and come out on the other side."

Out of all my siblings, Mason was the one to take my injury the hardest. He regrets not being there. Not seeing it sooner. The thing that no one could have predicted happening.

But what if I'm meant for more than just surviving? I want my life back.

It's hard to imagine what that life looks like. The life I had before my injury is gone. For the last twenty-one months, it's been nothing but surgeries and rehab. Focusing on building my strength in my leg so I can get back to the one thing I love more than anything else in the world.

Football.

It just might not be enough anymore.

All thanks to Audrey.

After reconnecting with her these last few weeks, my focus is shifting. Changing. Football has always been the center of my life. It was everything. It's been the default answer since before I can remember when people asked me what I wanted to do with my life.

It was always football.

What if that's changed? What if it's no longer the thing that drives me?

"We'd miss you, but home will always be here for you." Mason clasps me on the shoulder, pulling me in for a quick hug.

"Since when did you become such an emotional sap?" I try to cut the tension with my brother.

"Fuck off. I'm not a sap."

He totally is. And I love him for it.

"I'm glad to see you back to your old self. I hated not being there for you in the beginning—"

I cut him off. "It's not your fault. It's no one's fault. Just a freak thing that happened."

"I'm glad you were here though. If anything happened to you and I wasn't there…" His voice gets hard. Scratchy.

"I don't know if I ever said thank you."

"You didn't have to. We're family. It's what we do."

"Yeah, but you all did more for me than I could ever hope to repay. If it weren't for you guys, I'd probably be some sad sack with a fucked-up leg drowning my sorrows at some seedy bar."

"Given this a lot of thought?" Mason laughs.

There's the big brother I love so much.

He pulls me in for another tight hug before I open the front door.

"We're Winchesters. What did you think we'd do? Leave you on your own?"

"I'm lucky I have you guys."

So fucking lucky. My family means more to me than I'll ever be able to tell them.

This loud, crazy, interfering family is mine, and I love them like crazy.

And I wouldn't want it any other way.

# Chapter Seventeen

## AUDREY

"How did everything manage to get so spread out?" I let out a frustrated scream to no one.

Packing up to leave is never fun. Not when I'm leaving the person I only just reconnected with.

I knew my time here wouldn't be long. A way to train out of the spotlight. Being here has done more healing for me than I knew I needed.

Not only my leg, but my heart too.

Because things with Logan are different now. I held on to that anger for so long without even realizing it. Now that I know the real reason he left? It's hard to stay mad at him.

I throw a few more of my things in my suitcase before doing one more visual sweep of the small room I've been staying in. There's nothing to it. A small kitchen, a tiny living room with a loveseat, and a bedroom. Nothing to write home about. How has my stuff spread out so much in such a small space?

A knock at the door pulls my attention away.

Logan is standing there, snow sticking to his coat.

"What are you doing here?"

"Mind letting me in? It's cold as balls out here."

"How can balls be cold?" I ask, opening the door so he can come inside.

"That's what you're asking me?" He pulls the beanie off his head. His brown hair is a mess, but his eyes are lit up with excitement.

"Sorry. Why are you here?"

"Let me drive you."

"What?" He's stunned me speechless.

"To Denver."

"But why?"

"Because I need to get back for my physical with the team."

"You're doing it?" I ask.

Every time I asked Logan more about when he would meet with the team, he got defensive and never really answered.

"No time like the present." His smile is wide as he drops down onto the loveseat.

"And you want to come with me?" I sit down next to him, tucking my legs under me. Almost like a shield against Logan and the power he wields over me.

"I know you were planning to fly out in the morning to get there early, but it's not that far of a drive. Why not have some company?" He shrugs a shoulder like it's no big deal.

"And your family is okay with you leaving so suddenly?"

He waves me off. "They'll be fine."

"Logan, this is big."

"No it's not," he's quick to remind me. "Just any other physical I might have to take for the team."

There's hardly any room between us, but I close the distance, clasping my hand over his.

"It's okay if you're scared."

"I'm fine."

Men. Never want to deal with their emotions.

"When do you have to be back?" I ignore the elephant in the room of his looming physical with the team.

"Friday. Do you want the company or not?" He looks sheepish. Logan flips his hand, now holding on to mine.

Damn it. Whenever Logan would give me a look like that, it was hard to say no to whatever came next.

I should hate the hold he still has over me. But who am I kidding? I've always been a sucker for this man.

Always will be.

"Okay."

"Okay, yes?" His eyes are hopeful.

"Yes. I'd love the company."

"Yes!"

Logan grabs me around the waist and hauls me on top of him. The tips of his fingers find the sliver of bare skin showing under my cropped sweater as he squeezes me to him.

I don't think he knows the effect he still has on me. The smallest touch has me dizzy with lust. My breath is stilted as I take a deep inhale of Logan—the clean scent with the snow mixed in has filthy images slamming into my brain.

Logan's stubbled jaw brushes against my cheek. He tries to pull away, but my hand flies to his neck, holding him in place.

His dark pupils are wide with need.

*Is this how I look every time I see him?*

I haven't tasted this man in years.

Does he kiss the same? Taste the same?

My gaze darts down to his mouth where his tongue wets his bottom lip. Last time this happened—almost happened—Nash interrupted us.

Now, it's only the two of us.

Do I want to kiss him?

Logan doesn't make a move, and I know I have to be the one to initiate this thing between us. If I want us to be together again—however I want that to happen—I have to be the one to take the leap.

I don't have any control over my body as I close the gap of space between the two of us.

The second my lips touch Logan's, everything settles inside me. The thing I've been missing the most these last few years is him kissing me back.

I commit everything about this moment to memory.

The scratchiness of his jaw.

The way his fingers trace up and down my spine.

The groan as I lick my way into his mouth.

It's new and familiar all at the same time. My blood sizzles as I deepen the kiss. The stroke of his tongue against mine has my stomach swooping with desire.

I can't remember the last time I felt like this. I push up onto my knees, deepening the kiss. Holding on to his hair, I direct the kiss.

I take everything I want from this man. Everything that he's willingly giving me.

A shudder racks my body as Logan kisses a trail down my jaw, gently nipping and sucking at the skin there. The moan that escapes my lips is indecent as I cling to him. Bruising his shoulders as I sway into him.

I'm breathless as I pull away, my hands fisted tight to him. Whether to keep him close or push him away, I don't know.

"I need to pack." Logan presses one more soft kiss to my lips. "And from the look of things around here, you need to too."

"Right." I scramble off him, watching as he adjusts himself before standing.

With the race coming up this weekend and—who knows what will come after—I already feel our time together slipping away. This fragile friendship with him is more than I ever thought could happen.

Maybe it's all we'll ever get.

Logan grabs me before I can think too much on what happened.

"I'll pick you up at eight?" he asks.

"Eight." I nod in confirmation. "Logan?"

"Yeah?"

"This thing between us?" I wave a finger back and forth. "We need to go slow."

"Slow?" He quirks a brow at me.

"Slow," I confirm.

Logan takes a few steps backward, watching me as he slips his hat back on. The lust is gone from his eyes, a playful smile now etched across his features.

This is the Logan I remember. The one that made it so easy to fall in love with him. He didn't have a care in the world and would drop everything to come see me race.

"I can do slow, Audrey. You're back in my life after all these years, I'll give you whatever you need. I can be a fucking turtle if you need me to."

I laugh. "A turtle."

"A turtle. One who needs to get moving if he has any hope of hitting the road tomorrow."

"I'll see you tomorrow, Logan."

With a wink, he's gone.

Sending all of my emotions swimming through me. From that kiss to needing to take things slow with him. As much as I want to dive headfirst into things with Logan, there's a lot riding on these next few weeks.

Maybe slow is all I can handle right now.

Because what happens if I qualify for the games and Logan rejoins the team? We'll be split in two different directions. Again.

Slow is best.

Even if my heart wants more.

# Chapter Eighteen

AUDREY

"How on earth do you plan on spending the next day or so locked in a car with Logan?" Lily hisses over the phone.

"You know you don't have to be quiet, right?"

"What if he is there with you?"

"He's not."

I'm waiting outside for him to come pick me up, watching the snow that has been falling steadily for the last few hours. Spending the day's drive with him is something I'm now looking forward to.

Maybe my heart is softening toward the man I love.

*Loved.*

There is no current love for that man.

*Like,* sure. But love?

Even though we cleared the air between us and we seem to be moving forward together, I don't know if I can ever truly let myself be all in with him.

"Oh." Lily's voice is loud and clear on the other end of the phone. "Then how are you feeling?"

"It's fine."

"It's not fine. You were in love with this guy for years. Years, Audrey. Years."

She doesn't see the eye roll I give her. "I know that, Lily. Believe me, I know."

"So it can't be fine. Try again."

A smile tugs at the corner of my mouth. This is why I love Lily. She's one of the only people to call me on my bullshit.

"Would it be weird if I told you I was looking forward to it?"

"Of course not." Her voice is softer this time. "You two meant a lot to each other."

Things with Logan have been easier than when I first got here. The feeling of wanting to slap him is gone. It's better now. That hardness I felt toward him is gone.

It's like I can see the Logan that I fell in love with.

Not that I've been looking for that man. Or that he's still there. We've both changed. And I only have one goal in sight.

Qualifying for the games in a couple of months.

"You'll be there this weekend?" I ask her.

"I'll be waiting for you. Now, can I give you one piece of advice?"

"What's that?"

"Use condoms. There's no way you two aren't going to bang. Love you, bye!" she calls out, ending the call quickly.

Heat licks up my cheeks. Leave it to her to give me that reminder.

A big, unassuming black truck pulls up in front of the sidewalk.

"Looking for a ride?" Logan's face peers out the window.

"I don't know. I was told never to take a ride from a stranger."

Logan hops out of the truck and comes over to my side. With his ski cap pulled low, pink cheeks, and a red nose, he looks so good that seeing him makes my traitorous heart beat faster.

A tug deep inside my chest pulls toward him.

*Clearly it didn't get the memo we're taking this slow.*

"Well, it's a good thing we aren't strangers then." He winks at me. Hair curls around the bottom of his hat as he leans over to grab my bags. "Is this really all you have?"

"What?" I shrug a shoulder. "I wasn't planning on staying here that long."

"That's obvious."

Logan opens my door like the gentleman that he is.

"You ready?" He rubs his cold hands together, blowing into them.

Being in this tight, enclosed space with Logan is already messing with my head. The scent of him is over-whelming.

He always smelled amazing. I don't know what cologne he used, but it was embedded in every cell of his. It's why I still have one of his sweatshirts.

I hate that it comforts me still. But on the hard days, having that sweatshirt to throw on calmed me in a way I couldn't being to describe.

"Audrey?" Logan snaps his fingers in front of my face, pulling my attention back to him.

"Sorry. Let's go."

Not even two minutes into this trip and the only thing I can think about is Logan.

This is a really bad idea.

Logan

This was the worst fucking idea I've had in a long time.
Road tripping to Denver with Audrey?

I didn't think she'd actually say yes when I suggested it.
Flying would've been way easier. But somehow I convinced
her to say yes and drive down with me.

Both of us had to be there, so why not? She has a race
this weekend. And with my leg finally ready, there's no
sense in delaying the inevitable.

It's time to see if all my hard work over the last year
has put me in football shape.

It's the one nagging thought I've had throughout this
entire last year since I was cleared to start rehabbing. I
figure if Audrey is with me, maybe I won't be so distracted.

"Do you need any snacks?"

"We have a long way to go, Logan, and we just got
started. You already want a snack?" Audrey kicks off her
boots and crosses her legs underneath her.

"It's a road trip. You always need snacks."

Her quiet laugh is a balm to my nerves.

I never imagined Audrey coming back into my life.
Both of us are elite athletes with demanding schedules.
Even when we were together, it was hard to make time for
one another. Training required our full attention. We made
good use of what little time we had, but it was never
enough.

Now that she's back? I want to make room for her. I
know she's wary of me, but Audrey was always my person.

Who better to understand you than someone who is in
the same boat as you?

"Fine. Did you bring any snacks?" she asks, turning her
head toward me.

I chance a quick glance at her. The roads are quiet as

we leave town. Snow started early and it's coming down harder now. It was supposed to clear up, but I don't know if that's going to happen.

I'm only hoping it doesn't take longer to get to Denver than planned.

Or maybe I do. Would it be the worst thing in the world to be stuck with Audrey for longer?

"Check the cooler."

She shuffles around in her seat, leaning over the bench.

There's barely any room between the side of her ass and my face. So many inappropriate thoughts are racing through my head.

What I wouldn't give to be able to pull her into my lap and have my way with her. Maybe I'm just hard up and need to get laid, but I know it's more than that.

Sex with Audrey was always fantastic. There was nothing that was out of bounds with her. It was fun. And hot. So damn hot, just the memory of it has my dick hardening in my sweats. Sweats that won't do much to conceal it if I keep going down this road.

"Holy shit," her voice sounds from the backseat. "You remembered."

She pulls out the tub of cream cheese and bag of corn chips, a smile lighting up her face.

"How could I forget? It's only the weirdest snack."

"Yet, you love them." She cracks the lid and drags a chip through the creamy schmear before popping it into her mouth. "How can you not love cream cheese?"

Audrey does a little dance in her seat at her excitement.

"Feed me?" I plead.

"You were just making fun of me for liking these."

"Please?" I stick out my bottom lip.

"Fine."

She begrudgingly holds a chip out for me and I chomp

down on it. There's the smallest amount of cream cheese stuck on her finger.

I grab her wrist, sucking the pad of it into my mouth, licking off the extra cream cheese.

A blush creeps up her cheeks.

Fuck.

I should not have done that. Everything about this woman is making me lose my mind.

I told her I could be a turtle. Take things slow. But that isn't slow. Damn it. Audrey is too tempting for my own good.

"I forgot how good that was."

Or maybe not. Because damn, was that ever delicious.

Not even talking about the cream cheese.

# Chapter Nineteen

### AUDREY

"Are you sure it's okay that we keep driving?"

It's been six hours since we left Dixon. The time on the GPS keeps ticking up. No matter how far we drive, it seems like our progress keeps going in reverse.

The snow is thick now. With the ferocious winds, it's hard to see more than a hundred feet in front of us.

"We've got be in Colorado already, right?"

"We're still in Wyoming, Logan."

"Shit. Really?"

He glances at the screen in his truck, confirming what I just told him.

"I think we need to pull over."

"Keep an eye out for some place."

"I think there was a sign for a hotel a few miles back."

"Already wanting to get me into bed?" He quirks a brow at me as he signals to get off at the next exit.

"In your dreams."

We're supposed to be taking things slow. Jumping into bed with Logan? It's the exact opposite of slow.

"My dreams are a very good place, Audrey."

A sign points down the road for the closest hotel, five miles ahead.

It's a slow drive through the winding roads of the foothills. It's empty out here. The sky is gray, made lighter with the falling snow. I can't remember a time I've seen it come down like this and not been out skiing.

Logan is an expert driver, getting us safely to the small hotel tucked off the main road. Nothing about it stands out.

"Here is as good as anywhere, right?" He looks over to me, letting me make the final decision.

"I don't want to be out on the roads anymore."

"Then let's go."

Grabbing our bags, Logan makes a dash inside as I follow behind him. Snow is thick, banked around all the cars in the parking lot.

"Afternoon, dears. Can I help you?" An older woman is sitting behind the counter.

"Do you have any rooms for the night?" Logan dusts the snow off his sweatshirt. It clings to every bit of him.

"I'm afraid with this weather the only room available is the honeymoon suite." Her eyes are large behind her oversized frames.

"I guess we'll be taking the honeymoon suite then." Laughter plays behind Logan's eyes as I step up next to him.

Of course the only room they have is the honeymoon suite.

Being with Logan in his truck was one thing. Being in a room with only one bed?

I don't think any human has that much willpower to resist this man.

It's like the Wyoming Springs Motel and Spa had other ideas for my trip with Logan.

I wanted to take things slow with him. There's a lot of time and years between the two of us. Things that still need time to heal.

But slow just went right out the window as we step foot into the honeymoon suite.

"This is, umm…" Logan trails off, looking around the room.

"Where a serial killer plots his next victim?"

"Yes. That."

Logan drops our bags on the floor by the door. Wood paneling covers the entire room. A few framed portraits of the area hang on the walls. A floral print comforter that has seen better days covers the king-size bed. Fake roses sit in a vase next to the TV sitting on top of the dresser.

The cherry on top? A Jacuzzi tub sits next to the bed by the bathroom.

"Why the hell is there a tub in the middle of the room? Is that supposed to be the spa part of the motel?" Logan goes to stand inside it. "And why do I feel like I need my shoes on wherever I go in here?"

I peek over the side. "Maybe it's so the cleanup is easier?"

"Cleanup?" He shudders before jumping out of the tub. "Okay, if we die in here…"

"I'll tell your family you love them?"

Brown eyes study me. It's like he's looking right through me and can see everything I'm trying not to feel.

Where Logan is concerned? There are so many emotions all jumbled up that I'm having a hard time making sense of all of them.

"Something like that."

"It's really not *so bad*." I pull the comforter back before sitting down. *Just in case.* "It's a little lived in."

Logan laughs, grabbing our bags. "You always saw the bright side of everything."

"It's dry and warm. Not much more you can ask for than that."

Logan lies down next to me, kicking off his shoes.

"I'm glad we stopped. I'm exhausted from concentrating on driving in that storm."

"Sorry you had to drive."

Logan peeps one eye open at me. "At least we can still get to Copper Mountain before your competition."

Shit. The competition. It's the entire reason we're here right now.

And I forgot.

Because of the man lying next to me.

"You okay? You went quiet on me."

Logan sits up, dropping his chin on my shoulder. It's hard to breathe with him this close. Logan was always overwhelming to me in the best way.

I never thought I'd date a younger man, but once I met Logan, thoughts of him consumed me.

It was fireworks. It was like every cheesy love song finally made sense.

"I was doing a good job not worrying about the race."

"And now?"

His breath ghosts over my cheek.

"I mean, I'm still thinking about it…"

"What else are you thinking about?" Logan shifts, pulling me toward him. On instinct, I throw my leg over his and straddle him.

"Lots of things."

"Oh yeah?" He tucks a stray lock of dark hair behind my ear. "Like what?"

"This weekend. The race." My eyes connect with his. "You. Us."

"What about us?"

"Everything that's happened. It still seems surreal that we're here."

"I wish I could make up for the past, Audrey, but I can't."

"I know." I close the distance between the two of us, dropping my forehead to his. "But what if we…"

C'mon, Audrey. Just say it. Say what you've been trying to deny yourself these last few weeks since Logan walked back into your life.

"What if we what?" Logan drags his nose along mine. It sends tingles rushing through my body.

It burns hot and bright. I haven't felt anything like it in years.

Probably since the last time I was with Logan.

"I don't think I can do slow. Not with you."

"Are you sure?"

Logan's words seal it. The way he cares about me and what I told him I want. I want this. Want him. More than I could ever express to him.

I nod, my eyes not leaving his.

I take in everything about this moment, in this tiny hotel room in the middle of nowhere.

The darkness of his eyes.

His full lips.

The stubble lining his jaw.

It's the Logan I fell in love with.

Logan presses his lips against mine. It's the softest of kisses, but it sets me on fire.

A fire that I am ready to let consume me.

# Chapter Twenty

AUDREY

"I need you, Audrey," Logan whispers against my lips.

It's the best words I've heard in a long time.

"Me too."

I rock over him as his hands slide under my sweater. I'm tired of fighting the pull he has over me.

I want to be with Logan. Feel him inside of me again.

The kiss turns explosive. I'm not sure who moves first, but our mouths are hungry, needing more than the taste we got last night.

His tongue seeks out mine. Every time it touches mine, it makes me wetter. Amps up my need for him.

Logan pulls my sweater over my head. His touch is reverent.

"Have you always been this beautiful?" he whispers against the swell of my breast. "Fuck, Audrey. You're even sexier than I remember."

I wiggle my hands between us, grabbing the hem of his shirt and pulling it over his head.

"You're not so bad yourself." I trail my fingers up and down his abs. Relearning his body.

Logan is as fit as ever. And as I trail my fingers back up, my eyes catch on the tattoo on his side.

"You still have this?" I trace the penny tattoo on his side. The tails side of a penny.

"I could never seem to get rid of it."

"I guess that makes two of us." I shift ever so slightly, letting him see mine. The heads side of a penny.

His lips brush over the soft skin there. "I thought you would've gotten this removed."

"I could never seem to get rid of it." I smile down at him.

It's like the connection between the two of us was frayed, never broken. As evidenced by the ink we still have on our body.

Something we did on a whim in Denver one night.

Holding me close, Logan turns us, moving me up the bed so my head lands on the thin pillows.

His hands move down my body, touching each part of my exposed skin. It's feverish. I need more, craving his body.

"I wish I could take my time with you right now…" Logan bites down on his thumb. "But I don't think I can. Not now. Not when I finally have you again."

Reaching up, I link my hands behind his head and pull him close. "We have all night. We're not going anywhere."

"Thank fuck."

He closes the distance, sealing his lips over mine. Seeking hands. Exploring kisses. Every part of him is setting off a flurry of butterflies in my stomach.

Logan stands, stripping out of his clothes before pulling my pants down. I slide out of my bra so we're both naked.

He gives his cock a slow stroke. The way he's looking at me? It looks like he wants to devour me.

"Are you just going to stand there?" I beckon him closer.

"Depends. What do you want to do?"

Leaning closer, I wrap my hand around his. "Allow me."

I stroke his dick, loving how it responds to me. I lean closer to lick the leaking slit. Humming, I take him to the back of my throat. The salty taste of him explodes on my tongue.

"Fuck." His hands thread into my hair, locking me in place.

Squeezing his ass, I pull him in and out. We both set the pace as he fucks into my mouth.

"Touch yourself, Audrey. I want you nice and wet for what I'm about to do to you."

I moan, strumming my fingers over my clit.

"Such a good girl. Getting yourself ready for me."

His eyes are focused on where I'm touching myself as I slide a finger inside. I'm impossibly wet. The Logan effect.

I bring my other hand around, squeezing his balls. He always loved it when I played with them.

Still does by the way he thrusts into my mouth.

"Shit. I'm not going to last."

He pulls out, massaging my jaw before dropping down to give me a kiss. "Are you ready?"

"Yes."

He digs around for his wallet.

"Condom?" he asks, holding the foil pouch in his hand.

I shake my head. "No. All my tests are negative, and I'm on the pill."

"Mine are negative too."

"Then no condom."

"On the bed, Audrey. Ass in the air."

I hurry to do what he tells me.

His chest covers my back as he drops kisses along my shoulder. "So perfect." Strong hands are back to exploring my skin. "All I want to do is mark you so you know you're mine."

"Yours," I whisper, wiggling my ass as his cock slides through my crease. "I need you."

That gives him the go-ahead. Logan lines himself up and sinks inside. He's not slow, but pushes in steadily.

"Oh God!" I shout, widening my legs to take everything he's giving me. "Oh my God!"

My voice is breathless as he stretches me. It feels so good.

"You look so good taking me like this, Audrey. Fuck." He squeezes my ass cheeks as my pussy pulses around him. "You are perfect."

He presses his lips to my back as he lets me adjust. I forgot how well-endowed Logan is. Just on the bigger side of perfect.

I swivel my hips, letting him know I'm good.

It's even better than I remember. Each thrust has him pushing me into the headboard. I push up on my hands to take him better. Every pump is rocketing my pleasure to new heights.

His hand reaches under me to play with my clit.

"So wet for me."

It sends stars shooting across my eyes.

"So good. So good," I chant. "Don't stop."

"Never," he growls out.

He picks up the pace, slamming in and out of me. Every time I'm close to tipping over the edge, Logan pulls back.

"I need to come." I throw my head back and Logan fists my hair, pulling my body to line up with his. We're both on our knees know.

"Together."

I nod as he starts to move again. It only takes a few more pumps before I start to explode.

"Fuck!" Logan shouts, giving a few thrusts before he starts to come inside me.

I reach behind me, finding any purchase I can on his shoulders. It's like my entire body is floating away. This feeling is something I've missed.

It's so perfect, him releasing inside me, that I want to cry.

Except I don't.

I let Logan hold me as we both float through our orgasms. Because holy shit. It was one of the best I've ever gotten.

Eventually, Logan slips out of me, laying me on the bed.

"I'll be right back."

Every muscle in my body hurts in the most delicious of ways. I can't remember the last time I've been this wrung out.

Logan comes back, cleaning me up with a tender touch. He pulls back the sheets and tucks me in before sliding in next to me.

"Feel good?" he whispers.

"So good."

Capturing my lips again, he gives me a slow, stupor-inducing kiss. "You better rest up, Audrey, because I plan on doing that again with you."

"I guess that's the bright side."

"Bright side?" he asks.

"Of this little detour," I whisper, curling into his side. "Getting to be with you again."

Because one time with Logan reminded me of every-thing I had with him. And even though time has caused some scars to open and close, he's still the same Logan I fell in love with.

The one I've always been in love with.

One stop at the Wyoming Springs Motel and slow is out the window.

I want Logan Winchester. And I'll be damned if I let him go this time.

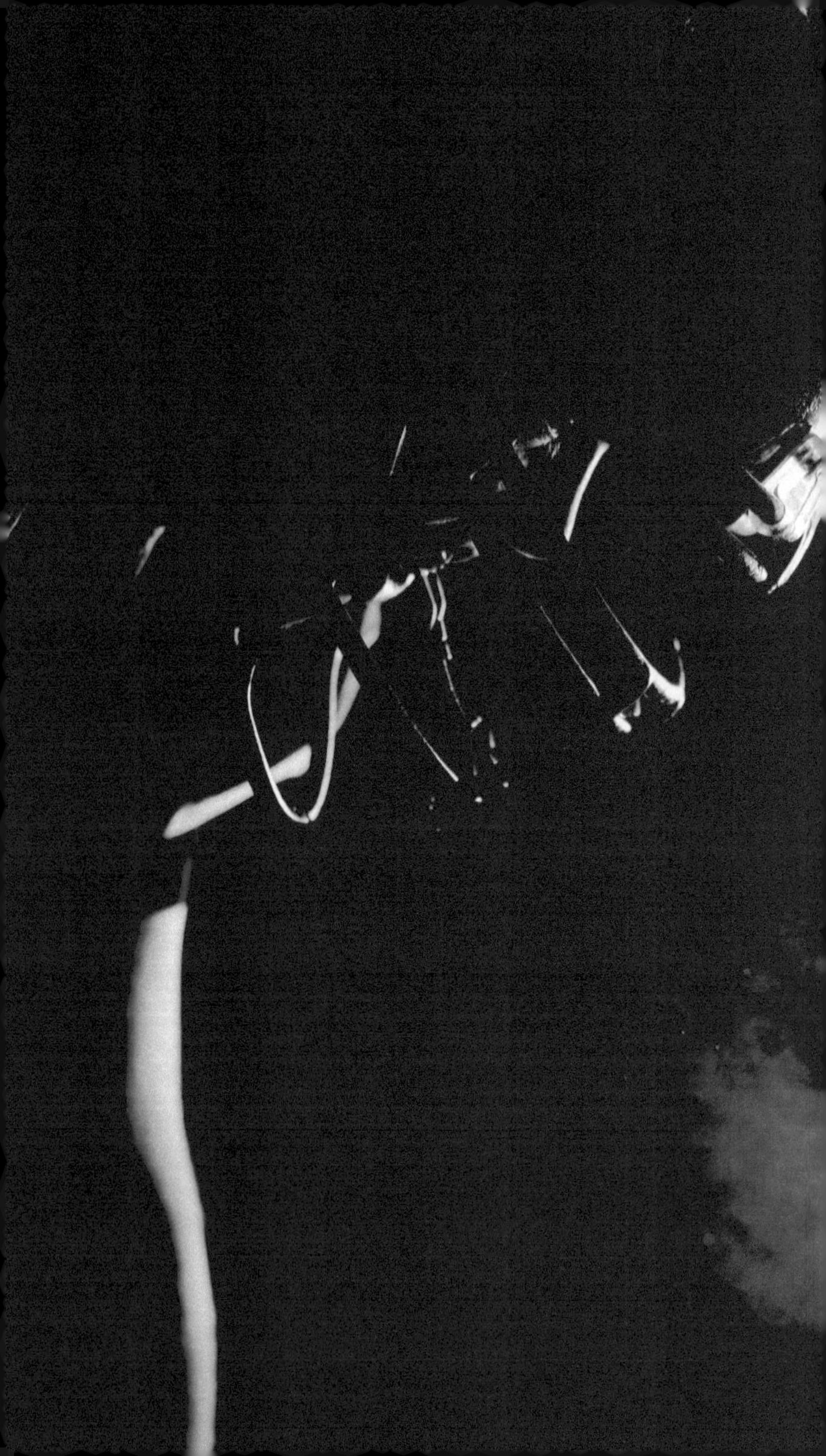

# Chapter Twenty-One

## LOGAN

"You're cheating!" Audrey bellows.

"I am not!"

"Yes you are. You're flipping the cards toward you so you can see what you have before throwing it down."

"I'm flipping them to the side." I show her exactly how I do it. "You're just mad because you're losing."

"We're neck and neck."

The stack of cards in my hand is bigger than hers. It's easy to see I'm winning. Neither of us enjoys playing poker, so a game of war it is.

We flip over the next card, matching kings.

"If you win this…" she trails off, setting down her next three cards before going to flip the next.

"How do I not remember you being this competitive at card games?"

"I'm competitive at everything, Logan. I just always beat you."

"Or did you?" I waggle a brow at her.

"Did you let me win?" That gets her going again.

"Why would I let you win?"

She throws her cards down and tackles me to the bed. The snow has finally stopped falling, but the snow drifts are the size of mountains.

We'll be lucky if we can leave tomorrow.

And having this woman spread out on top of me?

I don't mine one fucking bit.

"Logan Winchester, I demand to know if you've been letting me win all these years at our stupid games."

"Stupid games?"

"Answer the question."

Dark hair falls out of her ponytail, brushing against my face. Her eyes are bright. Fierce. Determined to get this answer out of me.

"Does the answer really matter?"

I can see her fighting the smile. "Yes."

Tucking a loose strand of hair behind her ear, I press a kiss to the corner of her mouth.

"I swear on my life, that I have never, ever let you win at anything."

A shudder racks her body.

"Not even the trail run?"

"Okay, maybe that."

"I knew it. You're such an ass."

"Am I? How can you blame me when I got to watch you run?"

She tries to push off of me, but I wrap my arms around her, starting to tickle her sides.

This is what I missed most. These moments with her. Getting to be ourselves. Logan and Audrey. Not the running back and Olympic skier that the world sees us as.

"Let me go!" she shrieks.

"I'm not going to let you go that easy."

Flipping us around, I pin her back to the bed, cards strewn all over the flimsy comforter.

"You're not?"

The playfulness in her eyes is replaced with something else. Something that has me getting hard in my sweats.

"I only just got you back. You think I'm done with you yet?"

Warm hands slide under my T-shirt. Short nails press into my pecs, and fuck, my dick is getting harder by the minute.

"Why don't you show me how *not done* with me you really are?"

I fuse my lips to hers, swallowing her gasps and moans. Sliding my tongue inside her mouth and exploring it. Learning her taste again.

It's only been what, twelve hours? And I'm already addicted to her again.

My own hands slide under her shirt. Warm skin meets my own as I push the soft material up and over her head.

With no bra on, my eyes feast on her ample breasts. The teardrop shapes and wide, dusty-rose nipples. I want to bury my face in them and not leave. Enjoy every single ounce of pleasure she gives me.

I flick my tongue over her nipple, getting it nice and tight. I love how responsive she is to me. She's a squirming mess.

I know she wants more. Can feel it in everything she's giving me.

But not today. Today, I'm going to draw this out for as long as possible.

I slip a hand down her pants and find the wet material of her underwear.

"You want my fingers, Audrey? Or my cock?"

She writhes beneath me, seeking out the friction. "Both. I want both."

"So greedy."

I lick a trail down her neck, nipping at all the tender skin there. Goose bumps break out in my wake. I press sweet kisses to her shoulder, all the while not giving her what she desperately wants.

"Logan," Audrey hisses.

"Yes?" I prop up on my elbow, staring into her eyes, bright with wanton desire.

"Put me out of my misery."

A lopsided smile slides across my face. "I didn't realize doing this with me was so hard."

"Ugh."

She throws an arm over her eyes. "I hate you."

Ignoring her, I drop more kisses on every inch of exposed skin.

"Now do you hate me?" I brush the material of her underwear aside and find her clit. My strokes are small and soft.

"Maybe not." Her free hand is fisting in the sheets. "I need more."

"Patience, Audrey."

Shifting around, I drag her sweats and underwear down her body so she's blissfully naked.

I can't help but look my fill.

"Are you just going to sit there and watch?" She drags her finger through her pussy, and fuck if that isn't the hottest thing ever.

"I might now."

Audrey spreads her legs, sinking one finger inside her. Her moans hit me and have me rubbing my hand over the bulge in my pants.

"Do you know how sexy you look right now?"

"It'd be even sexier if you join me."

"How can I say no to that?"

Standing, I drop my own sweats and boxers and take

my hard length in hand. My strokes match hers as I kneel between her legs.

It's so fucking hot doing this with her. Watching her get herself off as I jerk myself off. I roll my hand over the tip of my cock, spreading pre-cum down my shaft.

Audrey draws her legs up, wrapping them around my hips.

"I'm getting close." Her back arches off the bed.

"What do you need? My fingers?" I release myself, dragging my finger through her wet folds. "My tongue? My dick?"

"Your dick."

"I want to taste you."

Her smile is downright devious as I suck her fingers inside my mouth and push inside her.

I sink in to the hilt. I curse around her fingers in my mouth. That sweet taste of her pussy has me jerking my hips, sliding in that much more.

Swiveling my hips, I start to pull out. I'm in no rush, taking my sweet time with this woman. I'm glad we decided to forgo condoms because there is nothing like being bare inside her.

"Faster."

Grabbing her hand, I link both our hands and lift them over her head. "No."

"You're mean."

I slam inside her, watching as she throws her head back in pleasure. "Care to rethink that statement?"

"I'm so close. I need to come."

"I'll make sure you do. Enjoy it. I know I am." I give her a lazy kiss as I increase my thrusts. I want to take my time, but she's driving me crazy.

Our breaths mingle together as I keep pushing. Every whimper and moan of hers propels me forward. Sweat clings to my brow. I'm not ready for this to end. Except my dick is saying otherwise.

Tingles gather in my balls, heat shooting down my spine.

"Shit. I'm close. Come for me, Audrey."

I take her lips in a messy kiss. All pretense is over now. The time for playing is over. We're both desperately chasing our release.

"I'm there," she whines.

"Yes," I hiss.

Slamming into her once, then twice more, she comes unraveled.

"Logan!"

"Fuck! Audrey!" I hoist her leg around my hips and pound into her as she chokes my dick through her own orgasm.

The entire world could be ending outside, and I wouldn't care. Not with where I am.

"Fuck!" My neck muscles strain as my balls draw up tight and I start to come. "Holy fuck."

It might be the best orgasm in my life. I don't know what it is about Audrey, but every time is better than the last. Leaning down on my forearms, I hover over her. That face I love so much is now happily sated. A warm smile tugs at her lips. She pulls me down onto her, my head cradled in the nook of her shoulder.

"That was unbelievable," she murmurs.

"You've got that right."

Neither one of us moves. My dick softens, but I don't pull out. I don't want to lose the feel of her just yet. Something about this moment feels bigger.

Sure, we had sex last night. Multiple times.

But today? Somehow today feels different.

Like all our broken pieces have slotted back into place, fixing each other.

"We'll probably have to leave here tomorrow."

"I'm not ready to burst our bubble." Audrey drags a finger down the ridges in my spine.

"Maybe we can make this an annual thing. Come up to the Wyoming Springs Motel and Spa every year."

"You'd really want to come back here?"

I look around at the drab room. The wood-paneled walls aren't so bad. The jacuzzi in the middle of the room is weird, and it could do with a good scrubbing.

But how can I not love the place where Audrey and I reconnected like this?

"I'll buy the entire place today if it means you and I are coming back here together again."

*Together.*

Exactly how it should be.

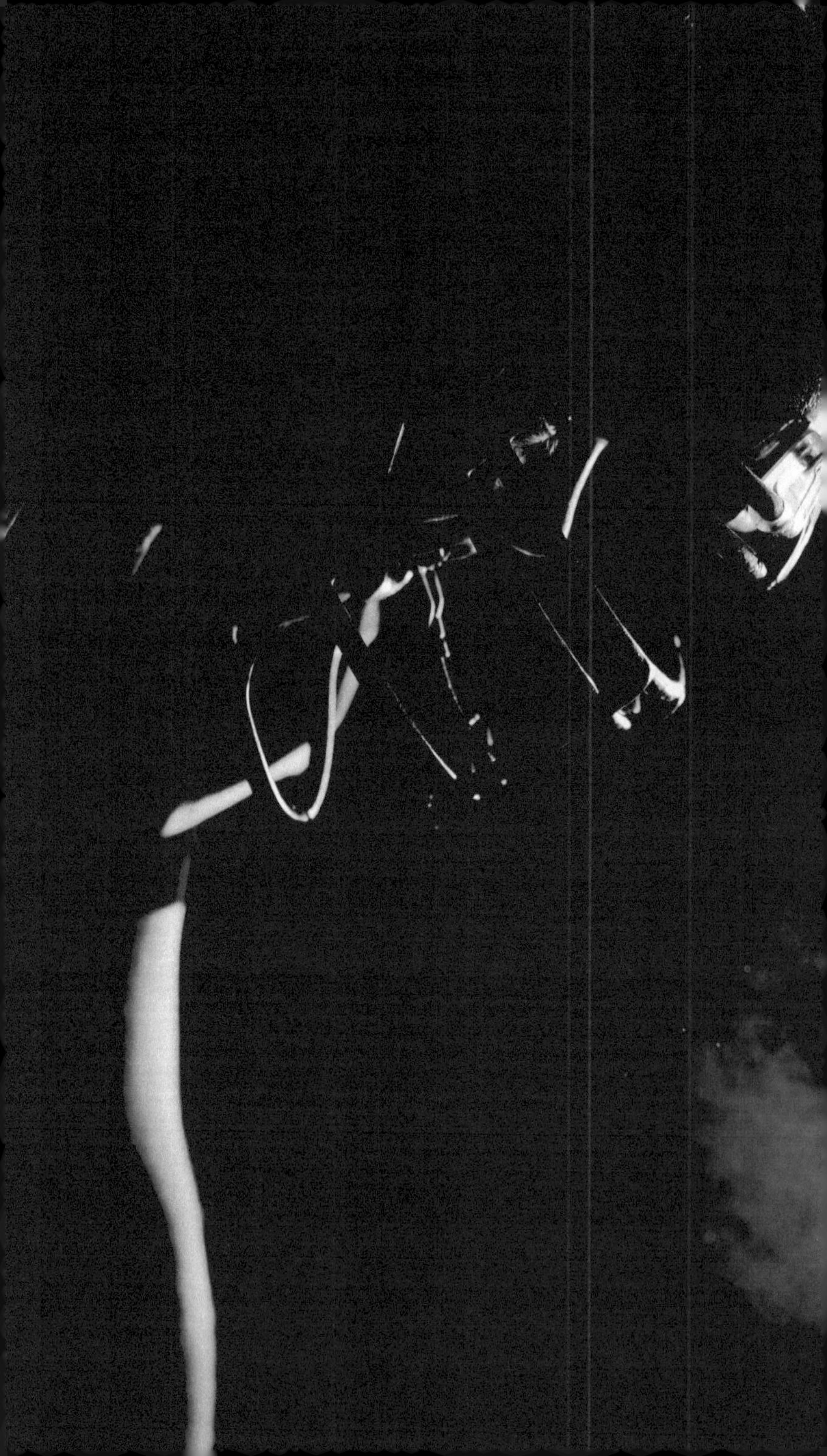

# Chapter Twenty-Two

## LOGAN

Today's the day.

The day I've been working toward for the last year. My workout with the trainers.

Every day, every setback, every early morning has been leading up to this.

After driving all day yesterday, I dropped Audrey off in Copper Mountain and came straight to Denver. I hated leaving that room. The real world is upon us, and it was hard to leave her, not knowing what is going to come for the two of us.

It's weird being here after being gone for so long. New buildings are going up all around me. It's like I don't even recognize this place.

I'm thankful that the team facility is quiet. With an away game this weekend, the team flew out this morning.

It's been a long time since I've seen the guys. I don't know how I'm going to feel seeing them for the first time, so I'm glad it won't be today.

They'd be nothing but supportive. They're my brothers-in-arms. We text, but during the worst of my recovery, it would've been too hard to see them.

Now? Having them here to cheer me on would probably get in my head.

Everything is the exact same as I remember it. Except photos of the team's Super Bowl win now line the walls.

I wish I could remember that day. But that entire week is a blur in my mind. Call it self-preservation, but I don't remember the hit or going to the hospital or flying home to Dixon.

None of it.

And through it all, the team has been amazing. Now if only I can get back out there and support them the way I do best.

Getting touchdowns.

"Logan. It's great to see you." The team doctor greets me in the training room.

"Great to see you, Doc." I shake his proffered hand.

"How's rehab been going?"

I'm sure he knows the ins and outs of everything that's been going on since I officially started therapy in Jackson. No doubt Scott kept the team apprised of my situation alongside my updates. Nonetheless, it's an easy way to make conversation.

"Good. Great." I instill more confidence in my voice than I'm feeling right now.

"That's great to hear. The team has missed you."

I wave him off. "Nah. Looks like Rodgers has been doing well."

"Doesn't mean we miss you any less."

"Glad to hear it." And I mean it. Rodgers stepped into my position with ease, as much as I hate to admit it. But if the team is winning, I'm happy.

Mountain Lions for life.

"We're going to start with some scans and then get you out on the field to see how you do. How does that sound?"

"Sounds great."

Everything hinges on today going well.

Because if it doesn't? I can kiss my future with the Mountain Lions goodbye, which is something I'm not yet ready to face.

"If you want to go ahead and lie down, we'll get started."

I hop up onto the MRI table. Thank fuck I'm not claustrophobic because I've had to do my fair share of these over the last two years.

The whirring of the machine is soothing at this point. It's almost calming the nerves I have, because after this, it's time to go on the field. To put everything I've done over the last year to the test.

My leg feels good. Strong.

I'm ready for this.

"Alright, Logan," the doctor's voice rings out over the intercom. "I'm done with you, so I'm going to send you out to the practice fields."

I'm moved out and hop off the table. A buzzing sensation is pulsing inside of me. I need a release for this energy.

And no better way than to prove to the team that I'm ready.

"You're ours now, Winchester." One of the trainers is gleeful as he meets me on the sidelines.

One field goal post stands on the opposite side of the smaller field. The Mountain Lions emblem on the wall between the uprights stares me down.

A few pieces of equipment are on the field, giving me an idea of what I'll be doing today.

"I forgot what sadists you were, working us to the bone out here."

"Made you a better player," he points out.

"Can't argue with that."

They detail everything I'll be doing today. Nothing that I haven't done before.

"Let's start with the forty-yard dash."

"I'm ready."

I line up, stretching my legs. I've got this.

The horn sounds and I take off down the field, pumping my arms to increase my speed. My leg feels good as I push myself faster. Harder.

I worked with Scott on this so often, he was ready to ship me off to Denver before I was emotionally ready.

Tilting forward, I cross the finish line. Unlike at the combine, there's no time clock to tell me how I did.

My stomach drops when I look over at the trainers. Their attention is on their stopwatches. They wear matching expressions—furrowed brows and lips pulled down.

Shit.

Both of their eyes look up to meet mine and I know from that one look.

This isn't good. I have no idea what my time was, but I felt good. Maybe it wasn't good enough.

Fuck. *Fuck.*

It can't all be over just like that, can it?

They send me through the rest of my sets. Running through the tackling dummies. Working on the ladder on the field. Practicing hand-offs.

Muscle memory kicks in and I do everything with ease. It helps quiet the now nagging thoughts in my head.

*What if my best wasn't good enough? What if this is the end of my football career?*

I take a swig of water on the sidelines as one of the team assistants comes over to me.

"We'll call you tomorrow to set a time to come in and discuss everything, okay?"

"Sounds like a plan."

"You should be really proud of how far you've come, Logan. Real proud." He claps me on the shoulder.

"Mind if I check out the locker room?" I ask.

"Have at it." He waves me off.

I blow out the nervous breath I've been holding as I make my way to the locker rooms.

My old stomping ground. The Mountain Lion on the floor. A wide open room with wooden lockers on every wall.

Still smells the same. Like cologne and sweat.

This place was my home for the better part of eight years. I gave everything I had to this team. Left it all out on the field. I prepared for every game like Alex taught me. Learned how to shrug off the defense from Knox.

I grew up here. Found a second family.

*Who am I without it?*

Tears wet my eyes, lip starting to quiver.

Fuck. Am I going to lose it here?

An equipment manager comes in, grabbing things from lockers. I don't need this person I don't recognize to see me have a breakdown.

I check the time. If I leave now, there's just enough time to head home and get cleaned up to meet Audrey for her event tonight. I was planning on staying here, but fuck it.

We only just got each other back. Even if I don't get football back, I'm not going to make the same mistake twice.

Because if I have anything to say about it, we're

together. No more breaks. No more countries and distance getting in the way.

I love her even more now than I did before.

And I never want to let her go.

# Chapter Twenty-Three

AUDREY

"Wow! You are a knockout." Lily whistles from her spot on my bed.

With the race tomorrow, there's a gala event tonight with all of the competitors. Something different, but my presence is required.

"Green is your color."

"Thanks."

The forest-green, velvet dress dips low in the front with a slit that is almost indecent. Logan would love it if he were here.

With his physical with the team today, I didn't want to do anything that could distract him.

Including having him by my side.

"How did you get out of the event?" I ask Lily, donning the last of my lip stain before smacking my lips together.

"Easy. I've already qualified." She flips through the magazine on my bed.

"Show-off."

"You love me."

"I'm beginning to question why." I roll my eyes. "How much press will be there tonight?"

"None."

"Really?" My wide eyes find hers.

"A few photographers and that's it."

Thank God.

I haven't run into Trent since getting back. With him not being here, it was easier to train today without having that added pressure of who is watching and waiting for me to mess up.

I let out a sigh of relief as the knock sounds from the living room. The car I ordered for tonight is here. No sense in walking across town in heels.

Grabbing the fake fur stole off my bed, I head out of my room. Except it's not the driver at the door.

It's Logan.

Looking sexy as hell in a black suit.

"What in the world are you doing here?" I ask as he steps inside.

"I couldn't let you go alone." He drops a kiss to my cheek. The stubble scratching against my smooth skin has my body aching for his. I didn't get enough of him in that hotel room.

"But the team. What happened?"

"I might know tomorrow, but I just had to be here tonight."

Deep brown eyes lock on mine.

"Are you sure? It's important."

"You're what's important," he's quick to answer.

Closing the distance, I press my lips to his, trying to show him how much his words mean to me.

Every worry I had about us starting this thing again quiets in my brain.

The kiss is chaste. Nothing overtly sexy, since we're

aware that we're not the only people in the room. But it's hard to pull back when Logan's hands settle on my hips, keeping me close.

"I told you I'd show up for you," he whispers against my lips.

I smooth the lapels of his suit, needing something to do with my hands. "You did, Mr. Winchester."

"You ready to go?" Warm hands cup my cheeks, bringing my attention back to him.

My breath catches in my throat with the way Logan is looking at me.

Like I hung the moon and all the stars.

Like I'm the best thing in his world.

Like he's in love.

The intensity in his stare has my stomach swooping. Maybe I blocked the past out, but I never remember him looking at me like this. With one gaze, he rearranges every cell in my body.

I never thought I'd get this again. But here we are. A chance to rewrite our history.

Together.

This man is it for me.

Standing with him now, I know I was stupid to try and believe otherwise.

"Audrey?" Logan chuckles. "You still with me?"

"Sorry." I shake myself out of my Logan-induced stupor. "I'm ready."

"You two kids have fun now."

Lily waves at me from the couch as we head out the door.

Now that it's December, the biting cold is here to stay. I snuggle in closer to Logan as he leads us to the car.

"How'd you know what time the event started?" I slide into the backseat of the chauffeured car.

"Easy." His smile takes up his entire face. "I found Lily and asked."

"Of course you did."

Logan wraps an arm around me, pulling me in close.

"Are you nervous for the qualifier tomorrow?"

"No."

"You don't have to lie if you are."

"I'm not." I mean it. "There's nothing like that race day energy, you know?"

"It's the same on game day. I know you're going to kill it tomorrow, Audrey. They won't know what hit them."

"Are you going to be there?" My voice is small.

"I wish. But I need to get back to Denver."

I sigh.

"If I could, I'd be there cheering you on."

"I only wish I could be there for you when you meet with the team."

It feels like it's starting again. I should be worried about the event tomorrow, but all I can think is I'll be here and Logan will be in Denver.

Apart.

Distance.

The very thing that drove us apart last time.

Are we doomed to repeat the past?

The thought makes my stomach sink to my feet.

Logan must sense it too because he's quiet as the car pulls up to the lodge at Copper Mountain.

"We've arrived," the driver tells us.

Guests are arriving in the circle drive of the stone lodge. It's lit up, like a beacon welcoming us all home.

A smile lights up Logan's face as he pulls me across the drive to an empty fountain.

"Want to make a wish?" Logan pulls a penny from his pocket.

I grab his hand but don't let go. "Why would I need to make a wish when I have everything I want right here?"

"Nothing for good luck?"

"Luck doesn't measure up to good training."

"You're a badass, Audrey Meyers."

Logan steps back, closes his eyes, and throws the penny over his shoulder into the empty fountain.

"What'd you wish for?"

We start walking toward the lodge where the reception is being held.

"Audrey, don't you know anything about wishes? If you tell someone what you wished for, it won't come true."

"My bad," I laugh. "How could I have *ever* forgotten?"

"It's a good thing you have me to remind you then." He kisses the crown of my head.

Everything about tonight is perfect as we walk into the rustic ballroom of the lodge. Logan on my arm. Drinks flowing. Skiers mingling with sponsors.

"It's almost unfair that it's an open bar."

"Why's that?"

"Because we're all competing tomorrow. No one can drink if they want to keep their edge."

Logan grabs a water bottle from the bar and passes it over to me.

"Maybe that was my wish."

"That I could drink?" I quirk a brow at him.

"That everyone else get so drunk they can't compete and you win by default."

My laugh is loud in the room. "Well now I know you definitely didn't wish for that because you wouldn't have told me."

"Fair enough. But it doesn't stop me from wanting the best for you."

"How are you so perfect?" The words slip from me.

I don't know how I got so lucky all those years ago. To bump into this man at the perfect moment at a football game.

I don't know if I could ever wish for anything more than Logan's presence back in my life. He's worth all the gold medals I have combined.

"I'd do anything for you. Anything."

Logan is at my side all night as I schmooze the sponsors and coaches. People are talking to him about his own sport as much as they are mine.

He's a natural with these people. The darling of the ball.

And before I know it, the evening is wrapping up. Thank God.

"Are you ready to get out of here?" Logan whispers.

I nod. "How about a gondola ride before we leave?"

"There's nothing I want more."

# Chapter Twenty-Four

LOGAN

I t's been a wild day.

After working out with the trainers earlier today, I rushed out of there like a bat out of hell.

No matter how good I felt, I don't know if it was enough. It's a fear I'm not yet ready to face.

My fate in the NFL.

Instead of sitting at home in my condo in Denver, I wanted to be here for Audrey. Even if only for a night.

I ask our driver to wait for a bit longer, then hurry back to Audrey where she's waiting by the gondolas.

The soft lights make her look like an angel. When she opened the door tonight, she took my breath away.

How did I get so lucky?

It made me realize I was never over her. No matter what I did to try and get over Audrey, it was all a Band-Aid.

She is it for me.

And no matter what happens in these next few days, I'll always put Audrey first.

She has to come first.

"Hey, sexy." Her voice is a beacon pulling me to her.

"Backatcha."

The car pulls up and Audrey and I step inside. With the event tonight, the team was offering rides to anyone that was here. And unlike the lifts back home, this one is enclosed. A warm, dark space hiding the people inside.

Audrey steps up to the windows as we start our slow ascent with a few other people.

They make idle chitchat as we ascend toward the top of the mountain. I perch against the railing, my eyes not leaving Audrey.

With every little jolt of the car as it carries us to the top, I track the sway of her body. It's fucking mesmerizing. I don't know how I thought I could ever live without this woman.

She's a part of me. Like the air I need to breathe.

Once we reach the top, everyone gets out to admire the view from the summit. The town is lit up like a postcard at the base of the gondola. As nice as it is, the only person I want to admire remains in her spot at the windows.

Now it's just the two of us alone in the car.

With the lights from the slopes giving off little light in here, it highlights Audrey's curves. Ones I have to have under my fingertips.

"Do you know how beautiful you look standing here?" I close the distance between the two of us, sweeping the hair off her neck. Her vein is pulsing.

"Why don't you tell me?" She tilts her head, exposing her neck to me.

"This dress." I fist the material, pulling it up. It's soft under the calluses of my hands. "Fucking delicious."

I nibble on her neck, hiking her dress up farther. Audrey arches her ass into me, nestling into my hardening cock.

"Do you know how these legs of yours drive me crazy?" My tongue darts out, tracing the throbbing vein, tasting her delicious skin. "I used to imagine them wrapped around my head as you sat on my face."

Audrey whimpers. "Tell me more."

"Yours hands would be twisted in my hair."

"Like this?" Her hands thread back into my short strands, pulling on them.

"Oh yeah." I bite down on her neck, licking the sting away.

"What next?"

The slopes come into view as we leave the station behind us.

"I'd flip you onto your stomach. I wouldn't let you come until it's on my cock."

"I love feeling you come inside me."

"Yeah?"

"I love feeling it between my legs," she purrs.

Fucking *purrs*.

All I want to do is fuck her here. But we don't have time. Ten minutes at the most, if I'm really lucky.

"Are you trying to drive me crazy?" I thrust my hips against her.

"It's how you make me feel."

My hand travels up the outside of her thigh. All that smooth skin is driving me wild. But when I get to her hip bone and feel nothing?

It makes me want to flip her around and pound into her.

"Are you going commando, Audrey?"

She nods. Covering her hand with mine, she drags it over, meeting the wet folds of her pussy.

"I couldn't have panty lines showing, now could I?"

"If only we had more time…" I trail off, going back to laving her neck with attention.

"What can you do now?"

The gondola slows, for what I can only assume is more people getting on and off.

Not the kind of getting off we're doing.

"I'm going to make you come on my fingers." I slip one inside, feeling how wet she is for me. "Have you been like this all night?"

"No."

"No?" I pull back slightly.

Her brown eyes are heavy-lidded with lust.

"I've been on edge like this since I walked into that damn gym. How is it you always have this effect on me?"

Pulling the neck of her dress down, I bite into the soft skin there. Marking her as mine. Because after that confession, how can I not?

"You make me feel the exact same way, Audrey."

"You've been walking around with a hard-on since I came back?"

"Well, not quite," I laugh. "That would be inappropriate."

"Maybe that's something I can take care of later?"

Audrey squeezes my finger as I pump it in and out of her. She takes me easily. It has me imagining it's my dick.

"Make me come first, and I'll make you come later." She throws her head back on my shoulder, grinding down on my hand. "That feels so good."

The lights from the lift reflect off the snow. Skiers zigzag their way down the mountainside.

"Do you think all those people down there can see us? What do you think they'd do if they looked up here and saw my hands under the front of your dress?"

I slip a second finger inside of her. Her hands tighten on the rail, going white.

"They'd probably crash."

My other hand sneaks between the fabric of her dress and bra, cupping her breast. Her nipple is hard. I love feeling what I do to this woman.

"Look at them." My words are a demand. Her head tips forward. "Going about their night without a care in the world. Not knowing what we're doing up here."

"Not knowing that you're about to give me the best orgasm of my life."

She hunches over, holding onto the railing with clenched fists. Knuckles white as I increase my pace.

We're getting closer and closer to reaching the bottom of the mountain. If she doesn't come soon...

The heel of my hand presses down on her clit. She's close. I can feel it with how tight she's strangling my fingers.

I sink my teeth into her neck, marking her again. I want to see the proof that this woman is mine.

"Come on, baby." I tug her earlobe between my teeth. Tweak her nipple. Curve my fingers inside of her and feel her start to shudder.

"Logan!" she shouts, coming unglued. "Holy shit!"

She holds my hand still inside of her as she rides out the waves of her pleasure.

Chest heaving. Nipple still hard under my touch. My hand drenched with her release.

Fuck. It's enough to make me almost come in my pants.

I hold her close as she shakes in my arms. My lips press warm kisses and words of praise against her neck.

"So good, Audrey. So fucking good."

The station is in sight, and the doors will open soon. I

pull my hand out, and she spins to face me as I suck her release from my fingers.

"As sweet as I remember," I groan. "So fucking good."

Her lips are swollen as I step closer, swiping my thumb across them. She sucks my digit into her mouth. Warm and hot, sending need spiraling through me.

I could pass out with how this woman is making me feel right now.

"You have never looked so sexy, Audrey." My voice is coated with want. No, a need so fierce I've never felt anything like it.

Audrey is the only one that has ever made me feel like this. Dizzy with lust. I can't wait until we get out of this tiny car and back to her house where we can spend the rest of the night together. I have to show this woman exactly what she means to me. And I'm going to make damn good use of every minute.

Her cheeks are flushed, dress slightly askew. I wonder if anyone can tell she just had the best orgasm of her life in this tiny car. Before we step out, I bring my lips down on hers, sweeping her off her feet.

My dick is still weeping, not getting the attention he wants right now.

"Have a nice evening, folks," the attendant tells us as the door opens and we step off. "Hope you enjoyed the views. Great night out here."

My smile is downright devious as a blush spreads across Audrey's cheeks. "You have no idea."

## Chapter Twenty-Five

### AUDREY

Today's the day.

The qualifier to the qualifier. If everything goes according to plan today, I'm one step closer to getting into the Olympics.

A place I never thought I'd be after falling during a race with near whiteout conditions.

But today? I throw open the windows to nothing but blue skies and sunshine.

The perfect day for a race.

"You ready?" Lily bounds into my room looking as chipper as ever.

"Couldn't have asked for a better day."

She gives me a once-over. "You look far too calm for today. I thought I'd be talking you down off the ledge."

Crossing the room, I sit on the bed next to her and grab her coffee and take a gulp.

"I'm perfectly relaxed. I've done this a million times before. No sense in stressing now."

Not to mention everything Logan and I did last night.

I didn't want him to leave. I wanted him by my side today. With him expecting a call from the team for a meeting, he needed to be in Denver.

I know his future hinges on this meeting with the team. I wanted to be there for him more than anything.

There is nothing worse than the fear of having your future slip through your fingers. He's not ready, and I'm not ready.

I loved watching him play the game. He lit up every time he was on that field. Picking up first downs. Quick cuts to get into the end zone. Celebrating with the team.

Logan is football. Who is he without it?

"You still with me?" Lily snaps her fingers in front of my face.

"Sorry. Thinking about Logan."

"How'd his physical with the team go?" she asks, leaning against my headboard.

"Fine from what he told me."

"You didn't get the details?"

"We were more concerned about other things."

"I bet you were." She waggles her eyebrows at me.

"Stop it." I shove at her.

"I want details."

"You get none. I need to get ready."

She rolls her eyes at me. "Sure you do. You just don't want to tell me about all the hot sex you're having now."

"Maybe after the race."

"I don't believe you." She pops off the bed and waltzes out the door. "Coffee is ready if you want some of your own."

"Thanks, Lil."

The rest of the morning goes exactly like any other race morning. Light breakfast, warm-ups in the gym, and two runs down an easy hill to get my feet under me.

By the time I'm in the gondola up to the competitors' waiting area, the jitters to get moving have hit me. Not to mention the huge grin on my face from what Logan and I did in here last night.

People from all over the world are at this event. Some are trying for their first qualifier, others are faces I recognize and am friendly with, having done this for almost half my life.

But now isn't the time to socialize.

Coach goes through the usual pre-race warm-ups with me. The conditions are perfect today, which means *I* have to be better than perfect.

As the skier before me enters the gate, I step up.

A moment of intense calm hits me.

Nothing else matters right now except getting down the mountain with one of the top times. I don't need to be number one today. I just need to qualify in the top eight.

"You've got this, Audrey," Coach hollers from his place near the gate. "Tight tucks and easy turns."

I nod at him, moving my goggles over my eyes. Tapping my helmet once for luck, I get in position.

Ready to race.

The horn sounds and I speed out of the gate.

Everything feels good as I head for the first turn.

Easy. Like riding a bike.

Fuck yeah.

After that, I know I have this in the bag. I couldn't be more thankful that the race today is on my home mountain.

I know every dip and curve of this monster. I've been racing it for years. Today, she's giving me everything she's got and I'm making her my bitch.

There's no better feeling as I race across the finish line to see that I have one of the best times of the day.

With only a few other racers behind me, I've secured my spot.

Congratulations are given to me from friends as I kick off my skis and head back to the waiting area with the rest of the team.

Coach eventually comes down, pulling me in for a hug.

"Great job out there today, Audrey. You looked great. Channel that next week and you've got this in the bag," Coach tells me as we head back to the training center.

"Next week?"

"You'll be going to Vancouver next week." He's not paying any attention to me—typing away on his phone.

"Wait, what?" That stops me in my tracks.

"The qualifier. It's the one you need to be at."

"I thought it was next month."

He shakes his head. "They moved it up. Something about lifts needing repair."

"When am I leaving then?"

"Tomorrow." He goes into his office without giving me anything else. "New course, so I want you to be ready."

Tomorrow? There's no way I'll be ready to leave tomorrow.

In the two days since I returned here, it's been full steam ahead. Meetings with the team. The competitors event. The race.

I've been out of competition so long, I almost forgot what this was like. The "be ready to go at the drop of a hat" energy.

Before, I could pick up and go with the best of them. With no attachments, if I was needed on the other side of the world the next week, it wasn't a problem.

No boyfriend or husband to worry about.

Except now, there's a lot more I'm leaving behind.

Logan.

And he's the very last person I want to abandon right now.

Heading to the locker room, I dig out my phone and call him right away. He picks up on the first ring.

"How'd it go? Results aren't showing online."

This is just like him. Tracking my race even when he's not here.

"I did it."

"You did? Holy shit, Audrey! I'm so proud of you!" I can feel his support from here. "I knew you would. Where'd you finish?"

"Third. But third is all I need."

"And the final qualifier is next month?"

I pick at a loose string in my sweater. If only I wasn't so nervous to tell him this. "Actually, it's next week."

"What changed?" He sounds as shocked as I was to hear that from the coach.

"They didn't give me the details, but I'll be leaving tomorrow."

He goes quiet. So quiet, I pull the phone from my ear to make sure he's still there.

"Wait, you're leaving?" His voice drops low.

"The qualifier is next week, and they want me to get practice time on the slopes there. I've never had a race there, so I need to get some runs under my belt."

"That's great, Audrey. I'm so happy for you."

Except he sounds the exact opposite of happy.

"Is everything okay?"

Pulling open a door to a cleaning closet, I step inside. I don't want to have this conversation out in the middle of the open where everyone can hear me.

"I didn't think you'd be leaving so soon. I'm going to miss you is all."

There's more to it than that. Logan is an open book with his emotions.

"Did something happen with the team?"

"Not yet."

"I'm sorry. I know you don't want to wait around for the results."

"It's okay," he tells me. "Where's the race?"

"Vancouver."

"At least you won't be going far this time."

"Do you think you'll be able to come?" I give voice to the one question I desperately need an answer to.

"Fuck. I don't know. I have no idea when I'll be meeting with the team."

My heart aches. I just got this man back, and it feels like he's already slipping through my fingers.

"Will you be here when I get back?"

"Of course. It's one race."

"One race."

"We can figure this out when you get back. You're going to crush it, Audrey. I know it. You will have the race of your life and be in those games with me cheering you on."

"Not if you're in the Super Bowl."

"There's no way I'd miss seeing you compete again. I've already missed too many." There's a rustling noise on the other end. "Listen, I have to go. But I'll call you every day, okay?"

"Okay."

"You're going to kick ass."

"Thanks, Logan."

Ending the call, I blow out a breath.

I feel more off than I have in a long time. This is exactly what I don't need right now. To be in a weird place with Logan the day before I leave for another competition.

Is it too much to ask that I get the best of both worlds? Who knew being in a relationship would be this fucking hard?

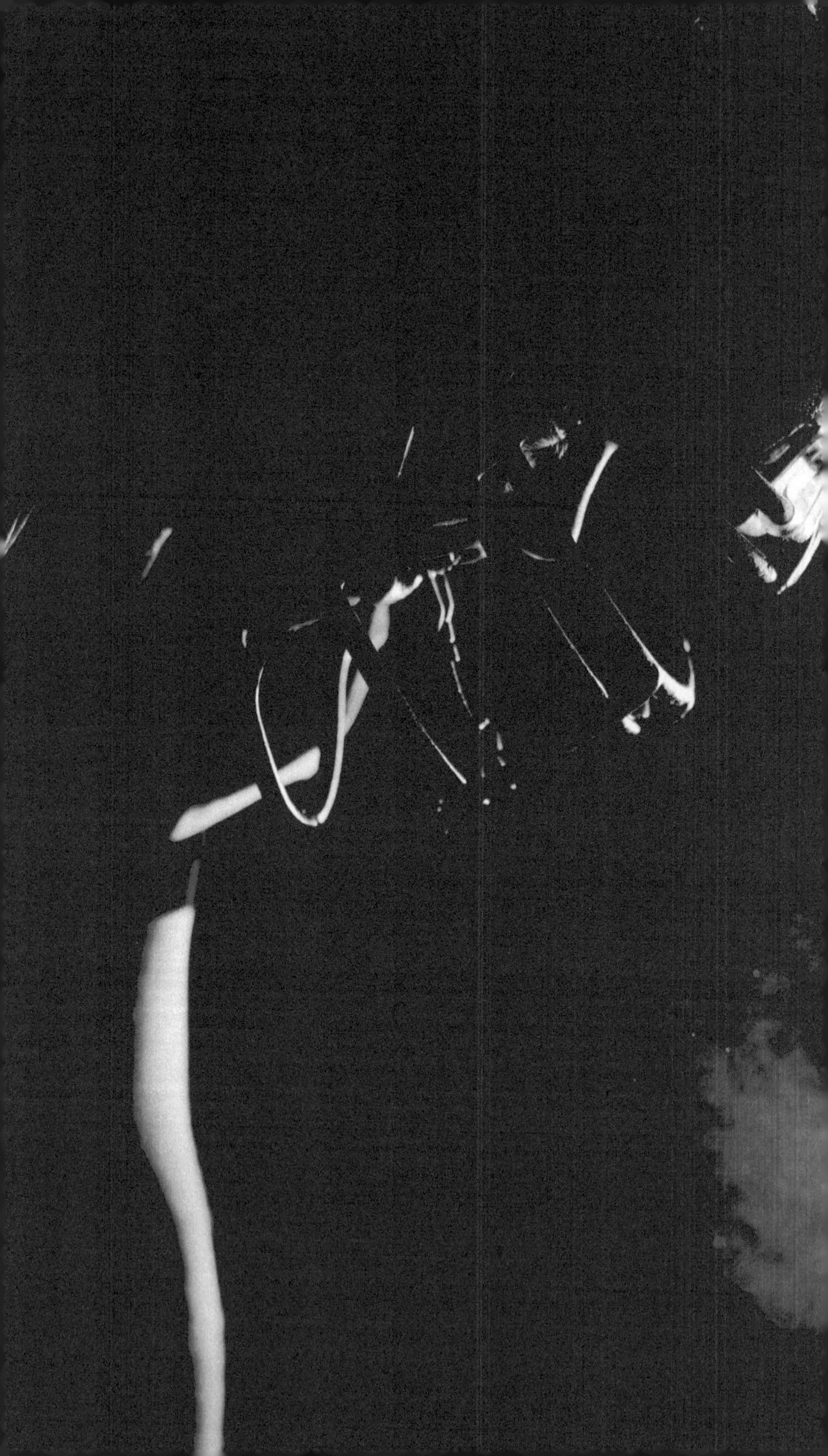

# Chapter Twenty-Six

## LOGAN

It's weird being here. Back in Denver in my condo. With Audrey having left yesterday, I'm all on my own.

And since she left, I've been ignoring my phone. The team doctor has been calling for the last two days. I keep telling myself that if I don't answer, my future isn't in jeopardy.

Stepping out onto the balcony, I take a deep breath of the cold air. I bought this place from Jackson after he moved in with Tenley. I haven't been able to give it up yet. It's been the one thing connecting me to this life. Being home in Dixon and training hasn't felt real.

And now? Now I don't know if my future will be here.

I still haven't said the words out loud to myself. If I don't, it won't be real.

Clouds are moving in from the mountains. The weather has matched my mood these last few days. I thought about checking in with my old teammates, but decided that wouldn't help cheer me up. I love the guys, but I think being around them right now, while my future with the team is up in the air, would do more harm than good.

And now with Audrey gone? I'm left with only the swirling thoughts of what that future holds.

The door to the condo opens behind me. What the hell?

"Logan? You here?"

"Gramps?" I walk into the living room, closing out the cold air that's been moving in. "What are you doing here?"

"Got a call from the team. They haven't been able to get ahold of you. What's going on?"

Shit. Of course they called him.

"I'm sorry, Gramps."

He sits on the couch, old bones creaking. "Don't be sorry. Tell me what's going on."

"I'm done. No more football for me."

It's the first time I've said it out loud. I haven't wanted to say it. I don't want it to be true. Football has been everything for me as long as I can remember. From peewee to high school to college, I've lived and breathed football.

Even for this last year, the end goal was to rejoin the team.

And now?

Now, for the first time in my life I feel lost.

I don't need a call from the team to confirm what I already know.

His stern eye meets mine. "How do you know?"

"Based on everyone's reactions the other day, I don't have the speed. The leg strength just isn't there."

It's the one thing I've been working toward this last year. Surgery after surgery. Over a year of rehab. All of it feels wasted.

Because my fucking leg isn't as strong as it should be.

"I feel like I failed."

"Says who?" Gramps crosses his arms, pinning me with a look that used to send me running.

"A gut feeling. I know that's what they will say. I won't suit up ever again."

"That doesn't mean you failed. You were given the worst hand that someone's ever had to deal with. You're here, Logan. To me, that's not failure."

I scrub a hand down my face, my emotions starting to get the best of me.

"What am I supposed to do?" I whisper. It's the thought that's been plaguing me since I left the facility.

"Logan, look at me." Gramps's voice is strong.

I finally look into his piercing blue eyes. Growing up, even with our eyes a different color, I was always told that I was the spitting image of him. That I was most like him. He was the one that was always at my football games. Even in college and the NFL, he always came to the home opener.

Gramps was the person I never wanted to let down. So to be talking with him now about the end of my career, it feels like I'm failing. Failing him.

"How long does a football player's career last?" His gray brows furrow as he looks at me.

I blow out a breath. "I don't know, maybe five years? Depends on the position."

He nods. "For running backs, it's about two and a half years. You were in the league for eight. You won a Super Bowl. How many people can say that?"

"Right, but—"

"Football was always going to end. It was never going to be something you did until you were forty."

"I guess not."

"Logan." Gramps beckons me over to sit next to him. "Your end might not have been on your terms, but you got more out of your career than most. And you're still here."

His voice is rough. It's not something we talk about much. It was a hard time, not only for me, but my entire family.

"You are not a football player."

"Not anymore."

Gramps claps me on the shoulder, grabbing my attention.

"No. Your worth has never been tied to you playing football. Did you make us proud? Yes, you did. Football was always secondary. But I was more proud of the man you became. No matter what you were going through, you were always there for your family. You're the best son, brother, grandson, and I couldn't be more proud of you."

Tears blur my vision.

"You've had a hell of a career, son. And you should be very proud of that. But you have a lot more to be proud of than just football."

He pulls me in for a hug. Having him here means more than I can ever admit. So much of my life has been tied up in football, that I didn't know what I would do without it.

Even though I won't be playing, Gramps being here, supporting me, makes the road ahead that much easier. Less scary.

"Thanks, Gramps," I mumble into his shoulder. "I love you."

"I love you too, Logan. Now, why don't we go get the official word from the team? No sense in delaying it any longer."

"I guess not."

Time to face the music.

THE TEAM FACILITY is just like it was when I was here earlier this week. I know there's a practice today because of Sunday's game. It's weird being here and knowing I won't be suiting up again.

The thought hits a little softer than it did earlier.

Following the intern through the building, they lead us to a conference room, where someone I haven't seen in a long time is waiting for me.

"Coach Brooks? What are you doing here?" I haven't seen him since the Super Bowl. Since I left the game.

"They thought you might like a familiar face here."

It confirms the bad news I'll be getting.

"How's retirement?"

"I get to spend my days with my grandkids. I can't ask for much more than that." A smile lights up his face. "How's your leg feeling?"

"Good. Most days it's good. A bit of soreness some days, but nothing I can't handle."

"You've been through hell, kid. I'm glad you're here."

"Logan. Glad you finally made it in." The team doctor and trainer come into the room.

Even though I know what this conversation is going to entail, I'm still nervous. Gramps gives me a nod before everyone takes their seats around the table.

"We're sorry, Logan. We really wish we had better news. We've talked with Scott and the team, and your leg is at max improvement. Taking all of that into account, the strength, speed, and agility aren't there. The risk of permanent damage would be too high."

"I understand."

"Other teams might give you a workout, but I don't foresee you getting another contract. One wrong hit and you could undo all the hard work that you've put into your recovery."

I shake my head. "There won't be any tryouts for other teams. Once you've played for the best, you don't want to go anywhere else."

The GM of the team stands, walking over to me.

"You've been a great player for us. I don't think we'd have this if it weren't for you." He hands me a small box.

I know exactly what it is before I open it.

My Super Bowl ring.

This was the one thing I didn't want while in rehab. I was in a dark place in those early days. The only thing I could focus on was surgery and not moving my leg to ensure I didn't do anything to fuck it up.

The reminder of anything football related would've set me back.

While I still wish for another one, I know most guys don't even get this one.

Snapping open the box, a gaudy, oversized ring sits on a velvet bed. The trophy sits in the middle with the Mountain Lions emblem behind it. The lights in the room sparkle off the diamonds. The score is on one side and my number on the other.

"Thank you."

"Thanks for all you've done for Denver. You're a Mountain Lion for life."

His words make my eyes sting as he leaves the room. Team lawyers are now in here to go over the rest of the logistics.

Contracts.

Retirement papers.

It's all straightforward. Lots of signatures to get everything filed—no sense in putting off the inevitable.

"You want to take some time here?" Gramps asks as the last papers are signed and everyone starts to file out of the room.

"Would you mind?"

"Not at all."

I hand him the car keys. "I'll see you at home."

"I'm proud of you, Logan. I always will be."

He gives me a quick hug before walking out.

Life-size photos line the walls as I slowly walk through the halls of the facility for the last time.

This place holds so many memories for me. I remember the day I signed my rookie contract. I nearly shit my pants I was so nervous. I was intimidated as hell with the level of talent Denver had.

"You weren't going to say hi to us?" The voice behind me has me stopping in my tracks. "Kind of a dick move, Winchester."

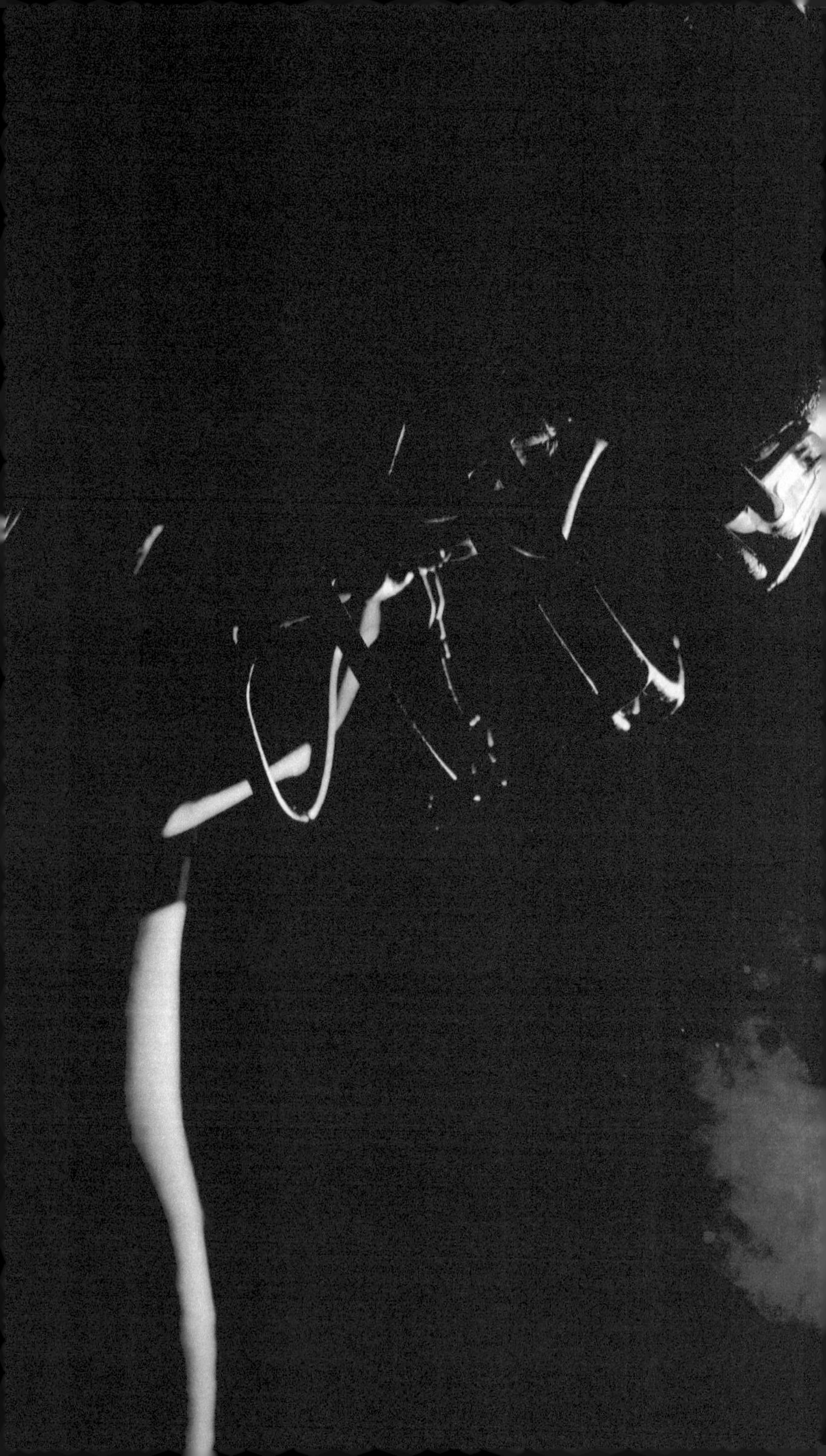

# Chapter Twenty-Seven

LOGAN

Knox, Jackson, Colin, and Alex are all standing at the end of the hallway, looking pissed at me. And from the looks of it, they just got done with practice.

"I'm surprised you're able to see me over Colin's ego." I laugh, heading toward them.

Shit. I haven't seen these guys in ages. While I tried to protect myself from football, having them here now puts a smile on my face.

"Not an ego if you have the skill to back it up." He shoves Jackson.

"No wonder he was trying to sneak out. Doesn't want to deal with you two." Alex walks around them, coming to give me a hug. "How have you been doing?"

"Not as good as you guys. Only one loss this season? Looks like I'm not missed around here."

"Don't let that fool you." Knox drapes his arm around my shoulder and pulls me into the locker room. "Colin cries himself to sleep every night you're not here."

"I'm sure he does."

The locker room is mostly empty now that practice is over for the day.

It's weird how foreign it already feels to be in here. This isn't going to be my place anymore. I won't be spending more of my time in here.

That'll take some getting used to. Even if I know it's for the best.

"Not the news you were hoping for?" Jackson asks, dropping down onto the bench.

"How'd you know?"

"You have the same look I did when I busted my knee."

"Yeah." I scrub the back of my neck. "I'm done."

"How are you taking the news?" Alex asks.

"Better than I thought."

"And how'd you think you'd be taking it?" Knox asks.

"I thought I'd be devastated."

"And now?" Jackson asks.

"Now, I feel okay. They said I could try out for another team, but my heart just isn't in it if it's not Denver."

"God, can you imagine if you got picked up by Vegas?"

They give a collective shudder.

No one—and I mean *no one*—likes Vegas.

"Not going to happen. It's Denver or bust. Looks like I'm the first out of all of us to retire."

"There is more to life than football," Jackson confirms.

Jackson knows better than anyone after injuring his knee years ago, during my rookie season. Injuries are never easy. But after battling back, I now realize it's the best decision for me. To step away from playing the game I love.

And I'm okay with it now. Talking with Gramps and Coach Brooks made me realize there is more out there for me than just playing football. I can do so much more. Hell, maybe even coach.

And with Audrey earning her place back on the team, I know she'll be busy traveling to competitions. Before, I could never go and watch her compete. It was always on TV or a shitty live stream.

With football out of the picture, I can be there to support her.

"Uh-oh. I know that look." Colin points at me. "Who is she?"

"Audrey."

"No shit, really?" Knox asks.

"Turns out absence does make the heart grow fonder." I can't hide the stupid smile on my face when I think about her.

If you had asked me two years ago where I thought I'd be, it wasn't here.

A busted leg that will never heal enough to play football.

The love of my life back.

"Love will always soften the blow."

"God, would you look at all of us? Complete saps," Colin laughs.

"They make it easy," Alex says.

"Not Frankie. She'll rip me a new one if I screw up on the field."

"The sign of true love." Colin bats his eyelashes at Knox. "But also, she's scary as fuck and I can't imagine her being my head coach one day."

"Don't let her hear you say that. I can get away with it because she loves me."

"Why? I don't know."

"You have time for a drink?" Alex asks.

"Don't you need to hit the weight room?"

"We're done for the day. You being back here calls for a drink."

Jackson hops up and grabs the small bottle of bourbon and glasses from his locker. It's nice to know that some things don't change.

"I won't say no to that." I take the proffered glass.

"So what's going to be next?" Alex asks, sipping his drink.

Taking my own sip, it burns on the way down. I wince. Shit, I haven't had this in a while.

"I don't know, but I have some time to figure it out."

"You'd make a decent stripper," Colin points out.

"I don't think there's a big market for male strippers in Dixon."

"Think you'll stay at home then?" Alex asks, ignoring Colin and cutting off that line of questioning.

"Right now? I think so."

Dixon has always been home. As much as I love Denver, it's not the place for me anymore. And as I'm starting to come around to the idea of not having football, Dixon is where I need to be right now.

"Maybe we can get up and visit in the offseason. Bring the families," Jackson tells me. "Got some room at that fancy ranch of yours?"

I laugh, swirling the brown liquid in my glass. "I think I can hook you guys up."

Colin bursts out laughing. "Can you imagine Knox on a horse? I'd give my entire paycheck to see that."

Everyone laughs at that. Except Knox, who flips Colin the middle finger. "And just for that, I'm going to make it happen."

The look on his face is less certain.

"I really would pay to see that too."

"And I'm ready to send you all back to Dixon and stay here," Knox grumbles.

"You make it so easy, old man," Colin laughs.

"I'm a year older than you. Jackson's the old man here," Knox points out.

Jackson knocks back the rest of his drink. "And speaking of being an old man, I need to get going. Noah has his own practice tonight."

"Is he playing football?" I ask.

Every single one of them cringe. Apparently it was the wrong question to ask.

"Hockey. I have no fucking clue how he decided on hockey, but I can't say no to that kid."

"Maybe he'll grow up and play for the Denver Ice."

One of Denver's other professional teams.

"Wouldn't be the worst thing in the world." Jackson shrugs a shoulder. "It was great seeing you."

He pulls me in for a hug.

"Yeah, don't be a stranger, kid," Knox tells me, pulling me in for a hug. "Just because you're not part of the team anymore doesn't mean we're not still here for you. We've missed you around here."

"Besides,"—Alex clasps me on the shoulder—"that's what family is for."

My chest tightens at their words. I shut myself off from them. Call it self-preservation, but it would've been too hard to hear about how they were doing and not be there with them.

"I will. I promise."

"You mean that?" Colin eyes me. "You're not like their kids and saying what we want to hear?"

"Hey!" Jackson slaps him across the chest. "My kid doesn't do that."

"He always tells me his dad is his favorite player. I know he's lying. It's really me."

"Yes, he is telling you exactly what you want to hear then."

More than the game, this is what I missed. These guys. They really did become like family to me. They took me under their wing when I was a lowly rookie and accepted me into their fold. Four established captains taking me in? I don't know if I would've lasted as long in the league without them.

"What are you looking at?" Colin asks, a smile on his face.

"I missed you guys."

"Who wouldn't miss us? We're the fucking best."

"Why don't you come to the game next week?" Alex asks. "I know Carter and the kids would love to see you."

"Maybe next time."

Because there's a girl in Canada that's more important than anything else right now.

# Chapter Twenty-Eight

AUDREY

"Conditions aren't ideal today."

"That's an understatement," I mumble.

I'm huddled in the competitors' tent at the top of the mountain, and the wind is howling. It started snowing a little while ago. Not just snowing, but the makings of a blizzard. But they won't cancel the event for a little weather. Their words, not mine. The first events have already ended, and they're grooming the mountain for us.

"You've trained for this, Audrey. You've raced in worse."

I want to believe him. But ever since I got here, it's been nothing but nerves. Not just because this is one of the last qualifiers to make it to the Olympics, but because of the way I left things with Logan.

Sure, his words said he was happy for me, but it felt forced.

Off.

I wish I had time to see him before I left, but I didn't. I've talked to him a few times, but I need to see him. If only to settle everything that's racing through my brain.

"I don't think I can do it."

The mountain looms large around me. Every other skier before me has either wiped out or crushed this run. With the swirling snow and wind, it makes visibility low.

Exactly like last time.

The time I crashed and tore my ACL, resulting in months of rehabbing in order to get to this point.

Fear fills every nerve I have.

*What if it happens again?*

*What if I don't have it in me to recover this time?*

"Maybe I'm not cut out for this anymore."

I kick off the snow that's gathering on my skis.

"What the hell, Audrey? Where is this coming from?"

"This is exactly like last time," I snap. "I'm sorry if it's getting in my head."

Getting angry with my coach isn't the solution here. But damn it, now I'm stressed.

"You've been training for months. You've got this."

It's true. My knee feels fine. Good, even. I've been doing training runs here all week leading up to this. I could do this in my sleep.

But after the injury, everything is making me take a pause. Second-guess myself.

I know I can't do this while I'm on the mountain. One split-second decision could mean the difference between making it down in one piece or tumbling down the mountain, unable to stop.

"I need…" My voice is breathy as I look around. "Fuck, I need…"

A commotion near the competitors' tent distracts me as someone marches my way.

A very familiar someone.

"Logan?" My heart catches in my chest. "What the hell are you doing here? You're supposed to be in Denver."

"I'm exactly where I'm supposed to be."

"But—"

He cuts me off as he stops in front of me, pulling off his gloves. "The question is, why aren't you at the starting gate?"

Tears sting my eyes, freezing against my face as the cold wind whips around us.

"I'm scared." My voice is small, quiet enough so that only he can hear me. "What if something happens?"

"You know what I think is going to happen?"

Logan takes a step closer to me, the snow crunching under his boots.

"What?"

Warm hands cup my cheeks, bringing my eyes to his. While mine hold nerves, his reflect the confidence he has in me. "You are going to have the best fucking run of your life. You are not going to let fear win. You, Audrey Meyers, are the best skier in the whole damn world, and I want you to go out there and show everyone else that. You got it?"

"But—"

"You got it?" Logan steps closer, dropping his forehead to mine.

"Yeah."

"That doesn't sound like you believe me."

"What if I fail?"

"Then you'll get back out there and try again." Logan presses a warm kiss to my lips. "Audrey, I love you. And I know this is scary. Believe me, I get it. I've been where you are. The difference between us is that you have the chance to get back what you love."

"What?" I don't miss his words.

"You can go out there and win another medal."

"Technically, qualify for the chance to compete for another medal."

Logan smiles, dipping his mouth closer to me. "Fine. But you still have the chance to go out there and show everyone that you have what it takes. That you're the biggest badass ever and that an injury won't stop you."

"Audrey. If you're going, we have to go now," my coach tells me. "You'll DQ if you don't."

"Give her a fucking minute," Logan growls.

In that moment, whatever fear I have is replaced with Logan's belief in me.

I can do this.

I can fucking do this.

Closing the distance between the two of us, I give Logan a quick, hot kiss.

Because there isn't a chance in hell I'm not making it down that mountain today.

When I find Logan's eyes, he's beaming at me.

And for the first time in a long time, everything settles into place. Both of us are exactly where we need to be.

"There's my girl."

"I'll see you at the bottom."

"I'll race ya." Logan winks at me and heads back to the gondola with other members of my team.

Dusting off my skis, I push myself over to the starting gate and listen to my name ring out over the loud-speakers.

The starter goes through the normal process, but I zone it all out. I've done this hundreds of times. It's what I do. It's what I'm *meant* to do.

Listening for the beeps, when the final one sounds, I'm out. My brain turns off and instinct takes over as I rush out of the starting gate.

The wind howls as I tuck down, bending through each turn.

The harder I push myself, the easier it gets. That heavy

feeling in my chest gives way to excitement at each gate I pass.

Every turn, every swish through the snow, makes my smile grow.

I already know this is going to be one of the best runs of my life as I fly toward the finish line. As soon as I cross, I throw my arms up in the air.

I kick out of my skis and wait for the final time to come up. The crowd is electric as we all wait.

The red numbers pop up on the screen.

Second place. With one skier left behind me, I did it.

I fucking did it.

I qualified for the games.

"Yes!" Pure joy pulses through me as my team runs over to me. But I have eyes for only one of them as I take a running leap into his arms.

"Holy shit! You did it! I am so fucking proud of you, Audrey."

Tears are flowing freely.

"I can't believe you're here." I bury my face in his neck, breathing him in.

I don't know how I ever lived without this man. I realize now I spent the years without him just trudging along and going through the motions.

Logan brought back that spark. The spark I needed to get past this setback and make it to my next Olympics.

"I love you, Audrey." Cold pinks his cheeks. With his hat, he looks as cute as ever. "Maybe I can become the official team motivator when needed."

"About that…"

Logan sets me down. "Later." He nods to the press behind us. "Go enjoy your moment. I'm not going anywhere."

That's the best thing I've heard all day.

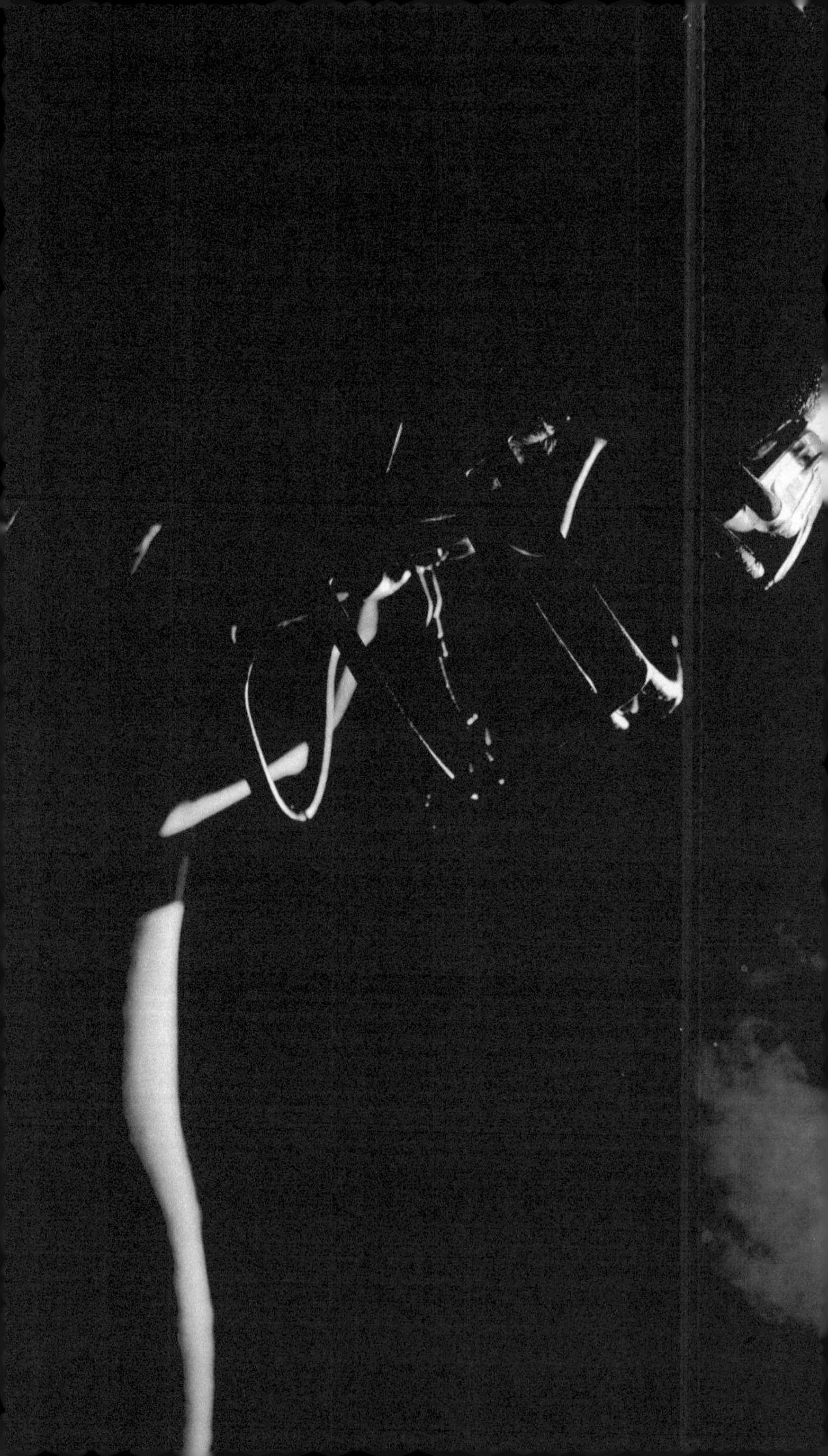

# Chapter Twenty-Nine

## LOGAN

The tick of the clock is the only thing echoing in the empty suite. It reminds me of being at home in Dixon, in the fancier suites we have at the ranch.

The small loveseat I'm sitting on faces the stone fireplace. A large bed takes up most of the room. The real focal point is the view out the windows overlooking the mountain. Night skiers are coming down in droves now that the snow has stopped.

After getting here at the last minute, I'm glad they had this room available. I had to shell out some serious cash for it.

I guess that's something I should probably start paying attention to. Now that the NFL money won't be coming in…

That realization doesn't hit me as hard as I thought it would. Because right now, there are more important things. Like the person now knocking at the door.

The leather of the sofa creaks as I jump to my feet.

Fuck. Audrey is even more stunning now than the day I met her all those years ago.

Her face is clear of any makeup. Her hair, still wet, hangs down her shoulders. She's casual in leggings and an oversized Mountain Lions sweatshirt. One I gave her years ago.

"Thought you would've gotten rid of this by now." I finger the worn gray material.

"This old thing?" She shrugs a shoulder as she pushes me back, stepping into the room. "Couldn't seem to ever part with it."

The lights are low as night has begun to blanket the Canadian Rockies. With the fire behind her, Audrey looks like an angel.

One I'm still not sure I deserve.

"What are you doing here?"

Closing the door, I saunter toward her. The loveseat in front of the fire is just big enough for the two of us.

"I thought it was kind of obvious."

Dropping onto the small couch, I pull her down next to me.

"Everything happened so fast with me leaving and—"

I cut her off. "Can we take a minute to celebrate the fact that you qualified for the Olympics? Again?"

Her smile could light up the entire world. I knew her fears. Hell, I lived them. Seeing her kick ass out there today was incredible.

"I can't believe it." Her hands press into her cheeks. "It doesn't feel real."

I pull her onto my lap. "I am so fucking proud of you."

Tears well in her eyes. "You're here."

"Audrey, I—"

Her lips cut me off in the sweetest of kisses. I don't know how I ever lived without this woman. I was kidding myself when I told myself I was doing the right thing by setting her free.

Turns out we both need each other to breathe.

"Tell me what happened." Audrey pulls away, but still stays close.

"I'm done. No more football."

"Just like that?"

I nod, squeezing her into me. Telling Audrey—someone who understands what it's like to lose the sport you love—is hard. Harder than telling the guys.

It's almost like they knew. Not playing football for almost two years? That's a hard thing to come back from.

"My leg isn't there. And no matter how much training I do, I'll never be back to one hundred percent."

"You can't get a second opinion?"

"I love you for trying to problem solve, but that's it. Another hit could damage it more than it already is."

"But you're okay, right?" I hear the panic in her voice. "Nothing that will affect your day to day?"

"I'm okay. I can't play football, but I'm okay." I drop a peck on her lips. "I really am. I promise."

"I'm sorry, Logan. I know how much you love football."

"Football isn't in the cards for me anymore. At least not playing."

A tear slides down her cheek. "I'm going to miss seeing you out there. You were an incredible player."

That has my heart catching in my chest. "I'll miss it. But I don't want to miss out on this."

"On what?" Audrey's voice is watery, and her deep brown eyes are locked on mine.

"You."

"Yeah?"

"I never want to be apart from you again. I've done that once and it was the worst fucking pain of my life. Never again," I whisper against her lips.

"But what about—"

I cut her off with a searing kiss. This is why I love this woman so much. We share in each other's highs and lows.

And for the longest time, I thought it was my rock bottom. But far from it.

"You, Audrey. You are all I need."

"I love you, Logan. You're my person. And I need you more than I ever thought possible. And some days that scares me."

Standing, I carry us over to the bed. "Not me. I'll never run again. Dixon. Denver. Switzerland. Wherever we go, it'll be together."

"Are you trying to write me a poem?" Audrey giggles as I throw her down on the bed.

"See if I ever write you one now." Brushing those dark locks off her neck, I kiss a trail from her collarbone up toward her jaw. Her laughs turn to moans.

"Will I still get this if you don't write me one?" Her legs widen, cradling me perfectly against her body.

I rock into her, letting her feel what she does to me. What she's always done to me.

"Oh baby. There's a lot more where this came from."

Audrey's warm hands slide under my shirt, lifting it over my head and tossing it to the side.

"Fuck, I love you." I kiss a trail down her neck, pulling her sweatshirt over her head. She's got nothing on underneath it.

I don't move. My eyes hungrily drink her in. Her tight nipples. An old scar on her stomach. The tattoo on her rib cage that matches mine.

Audrey is all I've ever wanted. From the first minute I met her until now, she's it for me. I knew the moment I laid eyes on her that she would change my life.

"Logan?" Her hands pull me down to her.

"Taking you in, is all."

We move together. Stripping out of the rest of our clothes, I waste no time sliding into Audrey.

It's perfect. So fucking perfect, I have to take a few deep breaths so I don't blow my load. The way she squeezes my dick lets me know we're both close. Neither of us are going to last long.

Audrey meets my every thrust. Her hands are clawing at my back. The bite of pain spurs me on. Long, hard pumps inside her. Drawing out our pleasure.

We have all the time in the world.

"You need to come," I growl. The heat from the fireplace has sweat sliding down my back. Hooking her leg over my shoulder, I start to move faster.

"I'm so close," she breathes against my lips.

I flick my fingers over her clit and she erupts around me, her neck muscles strung tight as she rides the wave of her release.

It only takes a few more thrusts from me before I'm tipping over the edge. It's not the most earth-shattering of orgasms, but it's the best damn one because it cements our future together.

Taking on whatever the future throws at us. *Together.*

Our breaths are one as we're wrapped up tight together. With Audrey's race behind us now, we've got a few days before we need to be anywhere.

"Are you going to come to the next race? I almost feel like you're my good luck charm."

I turn, facing her. "That was all you. You kicked ass today. I'm going to start my own cheering section for you at every race."

"Do I get a glittery sign?"

"Oh yeah. Is there such a thing as WAGS in the ski world?"

"What?" She laughs.

There's a lightness that surrounds us. Before my phys-ical—before Audrey's race—everything was so up in the air. It's like neither of us knew how we could move forward without knowing what was going to happen with the other.

Now? Now our future is clear.

We're together and that's all that matters.

"It's wives and girlfriends. But I can't be the only guy here. Can I start the HABS?"

She quirks a brow down at me. "Husbands and boyfriends?"

"Boyfriend for now. Husband later."

"Boyfriend doesn't seem like the right word for what you are to me." Audrey trails a lone finger down my jaw. It has my dick ready to go again.

I nip at the tender pad of her skin. "It doesn't. Not after everything we've been through."

The two of us have been through the wringer. Neither one of us have had an easy journey to get here. We've fought and clawed our way through hell to get to where we are now. Neither of us is the same person we were when we first met.

We've grown and we're a hell of a lot stronger now than we ever were then. Nothing can tear us apart now.

"You're my everything." Audrey's voice leaves her in a rush. "I really don't know what the future is going to bring —"

"I do." My voice is clear and firm. "You're going to kick ass in the next games. We'll make a home base in Colorado so you can train."

"No."

"No? What do you mean, no?"

Audrey shifts closer to me. "I don't want to be in Colorado. I want to make Jackson my home training center. I can do it anywhere and I want to live in Dixon. With you."

"Dixon, huh?" I drop a kiss on her nose. "You love it there that much?"

"I love it more because you're there."

Pulling Audrey into my arms, I snuggle down farther under the blankets. Warmth envelops the two of us.

"I can see it now. I'll take Coach's job at the high school. Be on the sidelines on Friday nights. Make sure you keep on a strict training regimen."

"But what about when I travel?"

"I'll be there."

"Even if you take on the coaching gig?"

"High school football ends in November, October if we don't make playoffs. And if I'm coaching, we're making it to playoffs. But if there's an important event, I'll be there. If they want me like Coach says they do, I think a missed Friday or two isn't the end of the world. As long as it's not playoffs."

She laughs. "I would never ask you to miss playoffs."

"Problem solved." I brush my hands together, like it's all set. "No reason to make it any harder than it has to be."

"Just like that?"

I lean closer. "Just like that. Because now that I have you again, I'm never letting you go. Someone's got to keep you on the straight and narrow."

Audrey laughs, so bright that it makes me fall even more in love with her. "Making an honest woman out of me then?"

I shake my head, brushing my nose against hers. "More like you making an honest man out of me."

"I love you, Logan. All I know is that whatever life we get to have together is the one I want."

"I love you, Audrey. And I'll make sure to do every-thing I can to support you."

"We'll support each other," Audrey tells me. "As long as we're together, we can do anything."

Together. That's all I ever wanted to be with her.

Looks like I finally got my wish.

# Epilogue



"This is quite the change from the Olympics."

Lily is sitting next to me at the last home game for the Dixon High School football team.

"You won't hear me complaining."

It's the perfect fall night. Bright lights shine down as the defense runs out onto the field in the second quarter. We're with the entire Winchester family, and no one is cheering louder than Willow.

After Logan signed his retirement papers with the NFL, he took the job of head football coach. I won't lie. I was worried that not playing would weigh more heavily on him.

He's a natural, like he was born for this job. The kids love him. The parents all love him. The entire town turned up for tonight's game to cheer the team on.

Because for the first time ever, Dixon High is headed to the state championship. All with Logan at the helm.

I couldn't be more proud of him.

It was a hard couple of months, splitting our time

between Dixon and Copper Mountain with my training schedule before the games, but we made it work.

Logan traveled with me as much as he could, and with the games behind me, I'm cutting back.

With three medals—two golds and one silver over the course of three Olympics—I want to spend more time here. Logan's even inspiring me to start coaching.

Make it the family business.

Who knew Dixon would become home for me?

"Maybe they'll give you a key to the city," Lily tells me.

"Sorry, Audrey," Layla pipes in, "you're a Winchester. As long as Brad is in office, there won't be any keys handed out."

"Because he's a prick," Simon adds before he pops a handful of popcorn in his mouth.

With the team honoring me tonight at halftime, Layla and Simon flew home from London for the event.

"Either way, we're excited we can all celebrate later." Layla beams with pride.

This is why I love living here. I was welcomed into the Winchester clan with open arms again. Logan's family— now my family too—means everything to me.

"It's going to be rocking tonight at the Cocktail," Gemma says.

"We even made you your own drink," Nash tells me.

"Wait, really?"

Peter elbows him in the side. "That was supposed to be a surprise."

"Oops?" Nash turns to me. "Sorry to ruin it."

"I don't think I've ever had something named after me."

"Logan approved, if that helps," Peter confirms. "But that's all I'm telling you."

Every one of the Winchesters gives Nash grief for spoiling the surprise, but it doesn't bother me.

I'm just happy to be here with all of them tonight.

"You know, you could still get that key to the city. You're not officially a Winchester yet," Lily tells me.

"If it means I have to stop hanging out with them,"—I throw my thumb over my shoulder where they all jump up to cheer the defense forcing a turnover—"it's not going to happen."

"Yeah, you are pretty smitten with them."

Logan and I have talked about getting married. Neither one of us is getting any younger. We both want kids and to start a family. But with my training and him starting his new coaching position, he wanted to wait.

And even though nothing is official, I still feel like a Winchester. They welcomed me back without a second thought. It's the big, loud, chaotic, and loving family that I always wanted.

I get it with Logan. The one person I truly loved and never got over.

Thank God training brought me back here. Logan makes me stronger. He makes me a better person. His love and encouragement are all I need in life. It pushes me on the days where I don't think I can keep going.

I don't want to think about a life without him.

The Dixon running back bursts through the defense and runs into the end zone for a touchdown just as the clock winds down to halftime.

"That's my cue."

Heading down the stairs to the field, I notice the entire Winchester family is coming with me. They haven't missed a single game yet. Gramps is the first one in the stadium. Always getting a seat in the front row to watch his grandson coach.

I don't think anyone is more proud of Logan than he is.

"You ready, Audrey?" Gramps gives me a peck on the cheek.

"I am," I assure him, even though nerves are settling into my stomach. Taking the medal out from my pocket, I drape it around my neck.

Logan is standing on the sidelines, not in the locker room with the team. I know this is the one time he's making an exception. The one thing he loves most about being Dixon High's football coach is being with the team during halftime.

His teammates from Denver were able to get away and come for his coaching debut. No matter what, Logan has a team around him.

"Welcome, everyone. We are thrilled to have Dixon's newest Olympian here tonight."

I still can't believe I took home silver this past winter. It wasn't the gold I wanted, but somehow, it felt better than anything.

Because this time, I had Logan at my side. I did it after coming back from a knee injury that I didn't think I would be able to overcome.

"Let's give a big welcome to Audrey Meyers!" the announcer booms over the loudspeakers.

The crowd is raucous as I step out onto the field.

I wave to everyone as they continue cheering me on. This town has done nothing but welcome me. And now that I'm taking a step back from skiing full time, I'm giving lessons at the local ski resort.

It's everything I've ever wanted in life.

Skiing and Logan.

Logan jogs out to meet me. With a beanie covering his

head, he looks, well, adorable. I can't believe that this guy is mine.

"What are you doing?"

"Remember this is how we first met?"

His eyes are bright, reflecting the stadium lights.

It was after my first gold medal. The Mountain Lions had me out on the field during the coin toss as an honorary captain.

It's where I first met Logan. I knew then, from that very first meeting, I was going to fall hard for him.

And now, all these years later, we're back together.

Better and stronger than ever before.

"I think I like this much better." Crowds have never been my thing. Cameras and reporters in my face at every turn? I prefer talking with the old ladies of the town when I'm out at the grocery store.

Their intrusive questions are easier to answer—like our plans for the future. I don't mind answering those.

Because they love Logan as much as I do.

"Want to like it more?"

"What are you—"

Logan drops down onto one knee, taking my hand. The crowd noise around us dims.

"Audrey Meyers, I love you more than I ever thought possible. You and I have not had the easiest of roads. We've taken a lot of hits over the years. But we're better together. You support me and encourage me and keep me going on the hard days. I love supporting you and showing you the same kind of love that you shower me with. And I hope that we can do that every single day for the rest of our lives."

Logan pops open a small box. A round, small yellow diamond sits on a gold band. It's the most beautiful thing I've ever seen.

"Audrey Meyers, will you marry me?"

I tackle him to the ground, planting my lips on his. We probably look insane out here, but I don't care.

"Yes! Yes! Yes!" I chant.

"Hell yes!" Logan squeezes me to him, dropping the sweetest kiss on my lips.

"We're getting married."

"Coach Winchester?" The ref is standing over us. "The game is going to be starting soon."

"Right, sorry." Logan pops to his knees, as light as ever on his feet, and pulls me up with him.

"Aren't you going to give me my ring?"

Logan pulls it from the box and slides it down my finger. Perfect fit.

"It looks beautiful."

"Not as beautiful as you."

I give Logan one more kiss as the team comes onto the field. "I love you, Logan."

"Not as much as I love you."

One more quick kiss from him and we're running back to the sideline. "Now, win this game, Coach, so we can celebrate tonight. I hear I have a drink named after me I need to try."

"Who told you?" Logan tries to look annoyed, but can't.

"Nash. But it's okay. As long as we're celebrating together."

"Is it too late to make a wish?" Logan whispers against my lips, giving me one more kiss.

"You didn't use your wish on me saying yes?"

Logan laughs. "I knew that would be a yes. I'm saving my wish for a lot of other things…tonight."

"Then you better finish this game, because we might have some time before we make an appearance."

"Yes, ma'am."

And that's exactly what he does.

Wins the game and then gives me the wish that I wanted most of all.

Him.

Logan Winchester. My future husband. My future. A quiet life in Dixon.

I wouldn't have it any other way.

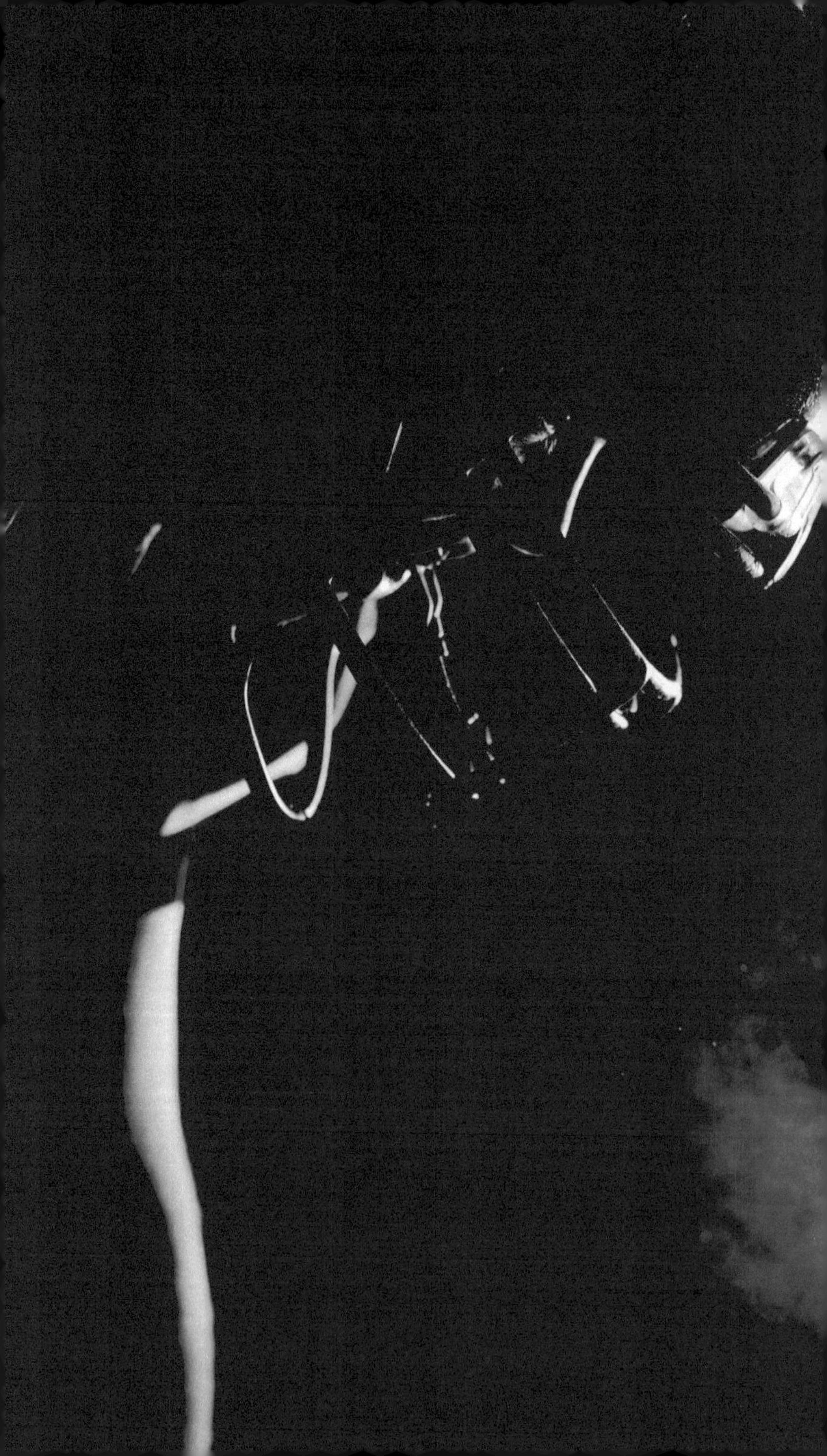

LOGAN

"I don't think I was this nervous before the Super Bowl."

"You weren't?" Lily asks, moving in closer next to me. The stands are packed. A nervous energy hangs in the air. Every athlete is aiming to end up on the podium. To feel the weight of a medal around their neck.

I'm so nervous I could puke. I want this for Audrey more than anything. "It's different when you're not the one in it."

Lily clasps a hand on my shoulder. "She's ready."

"I know she is. I just wish I could be up there with her."

The last few months of our lives have been nothing but preparing for this moment. For the Olympic medal run in the slalom. Everything has led up to this.

"Relax. She's got this."

Lily is the picture of calm. Soft snowflakes are coming down on the mountain as we're crammed together in with the rest of the US Ski Team. We celebrated her bronze medal run last night…by going to bed at a respectable hour.

Skiers from other countries have been coming down the mountain. Conditions are ideal today. It's making for fast runs. Which means Audrey will need to be damn near perfect to get on the stand.

I snuck out from my hotel early this morning to watch her practice runs. There's nothing like watching the person you love do what *they* love.

Audrey looked like she was flying down the mountain. I could see her grin from my spot in the stands when she was done.

I know she's ready.

But it does nothing to quell the nerves I feel for her.

"Would you stop?" Lily smacks my arm. "I can feel you shaking from here."

"Sorry."

"Next up, Audrey Meyers with the United States." The announcer's voice crackles over the speakers.

Here we go.

Audrey

"YOU READY?" Coach Anglia asks, slapping me on the helmet.

"I got this."

Sure, there are the usual nerves that come with a race, but today? Today I'm steady. I woke up the picture of calm. It might've had to do with sneaking away with Logan last night for a few hours before a self-imposed curfew, but I didn't want to risk screwing anything up today.

"Damn straight you do."

Conditions are as close to perfect as it could get. With

only light snowfall and no wind, it should be an easy run. After a few practice rounds this morning, I felt confident as I put on my team jersey.

In what is likely the last time that I'll be representing the United States in the winter Olympics.

I've only talked about it with Logan. I didn't want to focus on my retirement before the games. With the press surrounding the games, I didn't want to distract from my ultimate goal.

Winning a medal.

"Keep your turns tight and eyes up."

I smile back at him. "Got it, Coach."

"Now get out there and bring it home."

I'm called to the starting gate. My qualifying time means I'm toward the end with only a few people behind me.

Pushing my way through, I slip my goggles into place and watch the skier ahead of me. She's fast, but I know I'm faster.

Everything has led up to this. Watching the countdown go before the buzzer sounds signaling my start.

It's like my skis are a part of me. Each turn is crisp. Giving me an ounce more of a speed as I race down the mountain. The wind rushes by, echoing in my ears.

This is the feeling I love. Why I fell in love with skiing all those years ago. It's like I'm flying. Nothing can stop me as I go racing across the finish line.

"Yes!" I pump my arms in the air. I'm fucking ecstatic as I wait for the final time to flash across the screen.

Logan's shouts are heard above all the other chaos. Tears well in my eyes.

I don't think there was anyway I could have done this without him. He put his entire life on hold for me. To support me as I took one more run at a medal.

And it all comes down to this.

My time flashes across the screen. Second place.

Holy shit.

The nerves that I've managed to suppress are in full force now. There are still three skiers after me and any one of them could knock me out. Silver is not guaranteed.

I'm swarmed by my team and other coaches as I head for the waiting area.

"You've got this, Audrey."

"Way to go!"

"No way anyone can beat you!"

The congratulations do nothing to settle the butterflies in my stomach. Kicking off my skis, I watch as the next skiers come down the mountain. They're good. They wouldn't be here if they weren't.

But they both fall just short of my time.

And with one skier left, I'm guaranteed a medal.

Silver. Bronze. I don't care.

Because I did it.

I fucking did it.

I got a medal.

As the last skier crosses the finish line, it's confirmed. The skier from Norway won gold, I'm taking home silver and a skier from Canada took bronze.

A camera pans over to me and I can't contain the tears anymore. My eyes are searching for the one person I want to see more than anyone else.

He's running toward me, a smile plastered across his face.

God, I love this man.

"I knew you could do it!"

I leap into Logan's outstretched arms.

"I couldn't have done it without you."

"Bullshit. You kicked ass out there today, Audrey. I'm so fucking proud of you."

Warm lips find mine. This picture will no doubt be plastered across the sports pages later, but I don't care.

There is nothing better than getting to celebrate this win with the man I love. It isn't the gold I aimed for, but somehow, it's better.

Coming back from an injury and finding love wasn't something I thought would happen. I never dreamed this journey would take me back to Jackson.

And Logan.

"Audrey, you're needed for press."

"Go." Logan sets me down. "I'll be here waiting for you."

He drops another quick kiss on my lips before I'm pulled off. My eyes linger on him. On how proud he is. On how much he loves me.

It's worth more than any medal I could ever imagine having.

Time is a blur. From the medal ceremony to press to making it to the locker room to finally being able to leave and find the people I want to celebrate with most.

Logan and Lily are waiting behind my parents as I give them each a hug. They're crying just as hard as I am.

"I'm so proud of you." Lily pulls me into her arms as everyone looks on.

"Can you believe it? We both got medals."

"Because we're fucking badasses!" She yells.

Logan is talking with my dad, proud smiles on both of their faces. These are the people who have supported me the most. I'll never be able to put into words how much it means to me that they're here.

"Can I get a minute with our champion?" Logan

comes over to Lily and I, wrapping his arms around both of us.

"You already had your minute with me," Lily laughs.

"Har har." I roll my eyes at her.

"She's all yours, Logan." Lily drops a quick kiss on my cheek before giving us space.

I know the next few days will be nothing but celebrations, and I can't wait to have a proper one for both of us.

"So, how does it feel?" Logan asks.

"Like I'm on top of the world."

Warm brown eyes stare down at me with all the love in the world. It has my breath catching in my chest.

"I love you, Audrey. And I am so proud of you. You did it."

"Second place never felt so good."

Logan beams down at me, fingering the medal hanging around my neck. "Silver looks good on you, Audrey."

"Damn right it does."

As much as I wanted gold…silver really is the best.

Sign up for my newsletter now to stay up to date on all my releases!

**BOOK 16 IS OUT IN THE WORLD!!**

To say there were tears shed during Logan's book would be an understatement (I'm tearing up writing this right now!). Logan has been with me since February 9, 2022. He was never supposed to be in Roughing the Kicker, but I knew Dixon was in the works (I was going to write it after my royals, but a certain group of rowdy boys pushed their way to the front) and when I thought of how to connect these two worlds, Logan popped in as the newest rookie to join the Mountain Lions. From the day I wrote him into Jackson's book, I knew what his story would be. I knew what would happen in The Big Game and Yours to Lose and the journey he would go through to get his HEA. Did I sob writing his prologue? Yes, yes I did. His story was one of the hardest and easiest to write. It flew out of me despite what I put him through, and his HEA might be one of my favorites to date.

There's not much else I can say except thank you. Thank you for reading my books. Thank you for letting me continue to do what I love. And thank you to Logan for being so stubborn and giving me exactly what I needed to make these worlds work.

I hope you loved Logan and Audrey's story as much as me.

<3 Emily

# About the Author

After winning a Young Author's Award in second grade, Emily Silver was destined to be a writer. She loves writing strong heroines and the swoony men who fall for them.

A lover of all things romance, Emily started writing books set in her favorite places around the world. As an avid traveler, she's been to all seven continents and sailed around the globe.

When she's not writing, Emily can be found sipping cocktails on her porch, reading all the romance she can get her hands on and planning her next big adventure!

Find her on social media to stay up to date on all her adventures and upcoming releases!

# The Ainsworth Royals

Royal Reckoning

Reckless Royal

Royal Relations

Royal Roots

Royal Ties

# The Love Abroad Series

An Icy Infatuation

A French Fling

A Sydney Surprise

Love Under An Italian Sky - a newsletter freebie

Get the trope guide on my website, or

scan the QR code to read all my books on Kindle Unlimited

9 781961 359192